Love After the Storm

Wanda Benites

Contents

Prologue

One Year Ago

Cheer rang long and loud in the little pub in Stonebridge. The sounds of happiness echoed off the old pine walls in walloping gusts, flittered through the air in a merry, meandering breeze, and barked loud and boisterous like a gregarious beast on a contrastingly soft spring evening.

Ben Roberts gazed over the crowd jammed into the Plumber's Pub, taking in the many smiling faces, most of them rosy from the gushing overflow of booze. There was barely room to lift an elbow to pull a drink, but somehow the people managed to get heartily plastered in the name of love just the same.

The loyal herd had come out to support his sister, Abigail, in her marriage to Declan Fitzgerald of the Connecticut Fitzgeralds. Not that Abigail would enjoy such a label, being part of the "any-ones" of anywhere. She certainly wasn't known for her love of pomp and circumstance. Instead she was known for her fiery tenacity, generous spirit, and, now, for being the wife of one of the wealthiest men in the country.

A wife, Ben thought to himself. His sister was now a wife. Funny how quickly life could turn directions on you.

As the eldest male in the family, he had walked his beaming sister down the aisle and handed her over to the love of her life that afternoon. And, to his mind, his sister deserved all the love and happiness crammed into that after-party at their family pub, and more. Even after Abigail and Declan left on a private jet for their honeymoon, Ben dutifully continued pouring beer and whiskey for the motley crew of regulars, and he was as proud a man behind the bar as he'd been standing beside his sister in the ceremony.

The wedding itself had been enjoyable enough, though Ben hadn't attended any other weddings to compare it to. And he'd gotten through the whole tuxedo business without itching too badly. His younger brother Beckett had, of course, disappeared for a time with one of the perky blond wedding guests, while Ben had observed the elegantly attired crowd—the "important" acquaintances of the Fitzgeralds—with his usual, deep-rooted stoicism.

Beckett often referred to him as a stick in the mud, and—on most days—meant it in the most loving of ways. But Ben wasn't a stick in the mud. He simply knew what it was to ground deep and stand tall through whatever blew in his direction.

And because what had blown his way that day was a wedding reception, he'd found himself eating—and disliking—Beluga caviar, while comparing where he, Beckett, and Abigail had come from. The lavishly decorated, extravagantly orchestrated afternoon provided an anchor to look back at what their lives had been like not too long before. The three of them—the Roberts kids—had been dirt-poor outcasts from even the most trivial collections of society, had gone to bed hungry most nights, and had barely owned a thing to their name. And now the trio proudly owned and ran the Plumber's Pub—a local watering hole in their small Connecticut town. And their afternoon was spent surrounded by scents of flowers Ben couldn't have possibly known the names of, eating food fancier than any he'd ever seen, and being catered to by a staff of men and women clothed in white tuxedos and pressed gloves.

While they'd been on the verge of losing the pub the prior year, his sister's tenacity had ensured they not only kept the pub, but also could complete the construction renovations necessary to ensure the building was back in good standing with the health department. And somehow along the way, she'd managed to get engaged to her high school sweetheart who was, inarguably, the richest man Ben figured he'd ever know.

He thought it would change things, change the way day-to-day life ticked along, knowing his sister would never be poor again, but not much was different. And, because Ben was attune to changes and shifts in mood and meaning, there was a certain blanket of relief that soothed, knowing that his sister was taken care of.

In the monetary, sense, he added to his thought, chuckling as he poured three generous fingers of whiskey. His sister was extremely capable of taking care of herself. He'd once walked through the pub's kitchen door in time to see her physically tossing out a man three times her size. The drunkard had enthusiastically reached for—and made contact with—her ass after too many tequila shots. And out the man went, on the sidewalk—nose first—with little sweat from Abigail.

"You as drunk as I am?"

Ben glanced over to his brother who sidled up behind the bar. "No one's as drunk as you are," he told him, then slid the whiskey to their meat supplier who'd joined the celebration.

"Then why were you laughing by yourself?"

Ben eyed Beckett. "Because I'm just that hilarious."

"Yeah, you're a regular riot." In response, Beckett jabbed Ben with his elbow, on purpose of course, as he hefted a collection of to-go containers onto the bar.

The noise rose and roared—someone's story had caused fits of giggles and table thumps in the corner. Ben and Beckett looked toward the commotion, the two pairs of golden eyes sharpening for just a flash.

"Old Barley Bill, telling tales," Beckett announced.

"Same stories, same crowd, same laughs." Ben loved the reliability of it, the hold of knowing that the crowd of humans crammed into the pub would return, laughing and telling tales, day in, day out. It was like a baseball mitt that had been worn in through the years and fit your hand—the curves and movement of it—just perfectly.

Plus, it was springtime, Ben thought with a slightly whiskey-sodden, meandering mind. Which meant baseball season. And that, too, was just perfect.

"So what's all this?" Ben motioned toward Beckett's delivery of goods as he pulled another pour of pale ale.

"A to-go order."

Ben looked at his brother. "I can see that much. You went back and cooked in a closed kitchen during a private party?"

The two men were nearly identical in stature—both were built with the strength and solidity of naturally lean muscle, both featured chestnut brown waves of hair that tended to go unruly, and both had brilliant honey-gold eyes. But while Beckett's eyes broadcast the sparkles of his boyish charm, Ben's were warm and vivid with hints of darker waters that ran deep.

"Someone called with an order." Beckett lifted his shoulders in a shrug. "Couldn't say no."

Ben passed a beer along to the town's kinder-garten teacher who'd just arrived, then flicked a look at Beckett. "You mean a woman called with an order and you couldn't say no."

Beckett's face widened with a smile. "I'm a sucker."

"Clearly. What'd you make her?"

"Three boxes of whatever the hell we had left of all the food back there."

"Is that what she ordered?"

"It's what she's getting," Beckett offered, companionably.

Ever the responsible one, Ben retrieved the containers from the top of the bar and set them out of the way. "And I'm guessing you're leaving me to explain that to her?"

"That's why you're the one running the bar and I just run the kitchen. Well," Beckett corrected, "that's the setup for several reasons. You're better with customers and money, and I'm better with food and all things that happen behind closed doors."

"You should try closing the door more often. That girl last night moaned like a machine gun."

"That was fun."

"Not for me. Abigail and Declan better move out of the upstairs apartment so you can move into it. Then I won't have to put in shooting range earplugs when I sleep. The neighbors probably backed away from their windows, just in case."

"You know what you need?"

"Better sleep."

"Sex. Machine-gun loud, meaningless sex." Beckett reached for a handful of peanuts from one of the many bowls on the bar, tossed them in his mouth. Most of them made it in while the strays tumbled to the floor.

The glare Ben gave Beckett was one only a big brother could give.

"Come on," Beckett continued. "When was the last time you got laid just for fun?"

"I already clean up your messes when girls come in here crying, looking for you. I don't need my own messes on top of it."

"Have I thanked you lately for that?" Beckett tossed another peanut into his mouth but made a show of missing it, letting it hit his cheek and bounce to the floor.

"No, you haven't. And I'm not cleaning up after you or anyone else tonight. You're on cleanup detail, so that's a start in thanking me."

Beckett, who'd attempted to score a laugh from his brother, sighed at the lost cause. "Fine, fine," he lobbed out then slipped into the crowd.

Loud music chimed into the conversations, keeping the rhythm of the evening going. So when Ben glanced up and saw the newcomer swimming among the sea of people, he had a beat already thrumming through him. But at the full sight of her, the beat pounded harder, like an army of drummers in his chest.

She wore a powder blue sweater that accentuated her long black hair. And her eyes—a smoky gray color—struck him, piercing through his pulsing insides.

The noise hushed—or maybe that was only in his mind—and the people cleared away like a parting sea for a split second.

Like a dream, he thought. If he was thinking at all...

She was at once familiar and exotic, like a mystery he wanted to solve and solve again. The mass of shimmering hair, light eyes, milky skin, and a wide, generous mouth... He all but drooled on himself as she continued her approach toward him.

For just that moment, he forgot that he was behind the bar, that he was in charge of the collective ruckus, that they were in a busy establishment celebrating his sister's marriage. And instead, he was, in the most primal sense, merely a damn lucky man, waiting while a woman approached.

"I placed an order," she called out to him, breaking the spell that had scrambled his brain.

"Ah, uh," he fumbled, then held up a finger to wait given that he'd lost his ability to form words. And, he thought ruefully, it was probably too loud—in the pub and in his brain—to hear much clearly at the moment anyway.

Regaining his composure as he moved away to lower the speaker volume, he retrieved the containers on his way back and set them in front of her, then reached down below the bar for a bag to carry the load.

"Is it always like this in here?" she asked, her voice finding a way through the thick chatter.

And it was music for him—the melody of her voice. The way her mouth moved as she spoke just added to the tune, mesmerizing him. Her lips were naked, unpainted, and her top lip bowed perfectly, he thought. And her bottom lip made a pout that he wanted to explore, to feel the warm pliancy of.

"You'll have to come back and see for yourself," he told her, his lips tugging into a side grin. "You live around here?"

"As of this week, yes." She lifted her wallet to the bar. "How much do I owe you?"

"On the house." He slid the bag of food toward her, leaning in to the movement, and took in the scent of her. It was light, clean, with some hints of floral, he thought. And it was intoxicating. "A welcome to Stonebridge gift. Plus, I honestly don't know what my brother packaged up for you. It may or may not be what you ordered, so the surprise dinner is on us."

He wanted to ask questions, to get her talking and find out if she was married, or had a boyfriend, if she would stay until the party thinned out so he could have an actual conversation with her. But the woman looked like she had a goodbye on the tongue. And having watched his own mother disappear, he'd become acutely cognizant of those subtle signs, those small hints a person gave when their sights were set somewhere else.

"Oh," she said to him, puzzled. "Well, that's nice of you. Thank you."

"Trust me, it's my pleasure. You going to tell me your name? Since I'm buying you dinner and all," he finished. His golden eyes flicked into playfulness, though his gut felt a hard punch of serious lust. It really had been a pleasure—if even a shortly lived one.

"Kara."

"It's nice to meet you, Kara." He wiped his hand on the nearest dry rag before reaching over the bar to shake her hand. And when her slim hand met his, a quick bolt of electricity charged through him. "I'm Ben. Part owner of this crazy pub."

She nodded, her face polite, reserved. "Thank you, Ben. I appreciate the food."

He was right, he decided, watching her take the bag from the top of the bar. She itched to get out of there just as he'd itched to get out of his tux earlier that day.

But he was still wearing the slickly lined, black and white get-up. He'd somehow managed to make it through the events of the day and evening wearing the thing. And now, just as sur-prising, he was damn smitten with the woman who was a mysterious combination of day and night. Light eyes, dark hair. Sparkling scent, and a serious set mouth. Vibrant and, if he wasn't mistaken, a little sad.

On a charge, he rounded the bar, abandoning post and leaving a few regulars without their re-fills, then quickly pushed through the crowd to reach the door before she did.

Tugging it open, companionably elbowing back those in the way, he held the door for her to walk through.

"Thank you," she told him, a thin line of puzzlement creasing once again between her groomed dark brows.

His head dipped forward, acknowledging her words, while he enjoyed watching the woman's face. It was fascinating—it gave away nothing, yet there were traces of thoughts, skims of emotions, revealed for the taking if one paid close enough attention.

Instead of continuing through the door, she faced him squarely, and looked up at him. He was almost a foot taller than she was, so when her head tilted back, the chipper ceiling lights twinkled in her smoky eyes.

"This day was kind of a hard one," she said to him. "You made it better."

After a beat, she left through the door, walked swiftly down the sidewalk, then made a hard right at the end of the block and slipped out of sight.

People shouted his name from inside the pub, Ben was aware. But he couldn't move, couldn't take his eyes off the path she'd disappeared from.

And wasn't that a wonder, he thought, mildly registering that a beer was being handed to him.

Not caring where it came from, he drank deeply, grateful—for the beer, for the exchange with the woman. Kara. The woman of sun and moon, the woman who'd stung him like a lightening bolt.

And he wouldn't mind, he decided while draining the pint glass, being stung again. By her, he corrected. Not in general. General didn't interest him.

But Kara certainly did. Interested didn't even begin to explain it. Not even in the slightest of ways.

Or maybe there was just something in the air, something making his brain fog over from the abundance of sentiment and gushy matrimonial love from his sister's wedding.

Maybe.

But he would damn well find out.

"Now are you glad I took the to-go order?" Beckett stood next to Ben, holding his own beer, both men looking out to the town green and the tidy shops and shadows that lined it. The day had turned to night, with the streetlights of the town shining in a steady gilded glow just as the gaslamps had in the eighteen hundreds.

And for that breath, Ben wondered how many a man had stood as he was, watching with intrigue as a woman disappeared from reach.

When Ben didn't respond, Beckett drank from the IPA in his glass then continued. "So, you've met Kara."

Of course his brother had met the woman already, Ben thought grimly. The boy used his charm as though it were his greatest asset. And, quite possibly, it was his greatest asset. "You know her?"

"I know a little."

Finally, Ben glanced over. "Don't make a man beg."

"It could be fun. Especially from where I'm sitting."

"Spill or you're on cleanup indefinitely."

"Kara Keaton," Beckett said quickly, enjoying himself. "Moved here this week. Bought that old white dollhouse-looking place over on Maple. The one with all those willow trees in the front. The one we always thought was haunted."

"The house across from Stacie Fleck's place?"

Beckett winked knowingly. "How else do you think I know all this?"

"Naturally." Ben took a deep breath of impatience. "What else do you know?"

"She lives alone, at least as far as I can tell, and she's a widow. Her husband died a year ago. She's a writer. A mystery writer."

"You got all this from spending the night with Stacie Fleck?"

"I got all this when I talked Stacie into going over to Kara's place with me. A neighborly introduction."

Ben scowled. "You talked a woman into going with you to meet another woman?"

"Hey, it was a kind gesture."

"If you used your powers for good instead of evil, you'd be a superhero by now."

"Don't beat up on me, man. I went there for you. She's too old for me."

"How old is she?"

"Twenty-seven."

"That's only four years from where you're sitting."

"I wouldn't discriminate on that alone. In fact older women tend to know things. Maybe I will—"

Ben shot him a warning look.

Beckett bit back a chuckle. "Or maybe not. Plus, being a widow...that screams complex. I'm not into complex. That's your department."

Beckett handed Ben a piece of torn paper.

"What's this?"

"Kara's number. I asked for it when she called with the order. Figured it was her when she called. No other Karas around here that I know of."

Ben stared at it.

"You're welcome," Beckett told him then saun-
tered off toward whatever trouble he could find.

Sliding the slim paper into his pocket, Ben finally closed the door to the warm-toned evening
that still held hints of winter. It was that time
in the season that fluttered between the two
worlds—cold and hot, what was and what would
be.

Unable to look away just yet, he kept watch
through the paned windows in the door, looking
out after the woman who'd fascinated him.

A widow... He heard the word echo through
his mind. Must be a tough deal. Was that why
she said she'd had a rough day? Or was there
something else?

He didn't know the answers, but he sure as hell
wanted to find out.

Chapter 1

P resent Day

Kara Keaton opened her eyes to a cool spear of worry that accompanied the stormy dawn. Because that worry rose into fear faster than the morning light could lift away the darkness, she slid out of bed to begin her day with only a subtle silver glare showing the way.

Distraction was the name of the game when fear threatened battle. And after years of practice, Kara was a worthy opponent, armed with a creative mind, decisive momentum, and gritty humility.

Of course, after being knocked down by life, learning that her creative mind was a trusty weapon in her arsenal had been quite shocking. As a child, whenever she played war with her brothers, she'd armed herself with knobby sticks and a secret stash of acorns. If she'd tried to fight the likes of William and Liam Wyatt with her mind, she would've been laughed at then taken prisoner.

Likewise, if she tried to fight fear with sticks and acorns, she was also liable to find herself defeated.

The memory of family, the good times, led her back to the slippery edge of worry.

Coffee would save her, she decided. It was a good enough weapon for the morning.

She started down the creaky stairs of her ancient home. She'd renovated the hundred-year-old place, one project at a time. But something about those creaks that sounded as she made her way up or down the stairs made her feel like she was part of the home's history. These were her few contributory steps in the vast years of many. And if she fixed the squeaks, what stories would there be?

Then again, she was a writer so she appreciated the stories those stairs could undoubtedly tell. Similarly, if she fixed all the squeaks in herself, what evidence would there be of her past, her stories?

Still clad in thermal pajamas, she slipped her socked feet into her bright red pair of galoshes, tugged on a hat and tucked her long spill of dark hair beneath it, then walked out through the French doors, into the raging rain.

Coffee could wait. She'd battle her morning chores first, then claim her victory cup of caffeine.

Her warm breath was immediately pulled out of her, the clouded mist of it disappearing into the soggy darkness. Crossing her arms in front of her chest, she decided not to go back in for her jacket, and instead make the trip a short one.

Kara strolled through the rain—not terribly bothered by something as inconsequential as a storm—across the stone steps she'd hauled and set last summer.

Her brilliant white oak towered tall and proud in her deluged back yard, its spiny fingertips piercing the thick clouds that had gathered under the cover of night.

And beside the protective old tree was the modest greenhouse she'd hired a contractor to frame. Then, after researching the best materials to use and watching several how-to videos, she'd filled in the details after the contractor left. She'd done everything from installing the greenhouse plastic, to lugging in and filling the raised beds. Then she'd celebrated the completion by hanging a sign that read, "When Life Gives You Shit, Grow A Garden."

She opened the door to the greenhouse—which she'd stubbornly hung herself—as the ground shook under the threat of growling thunder. At the warning, she quickly scooted inside, half expecting the three-headed Cerberus to appear snarling through the mists, nipping at her chilled cheeks.

It certainly felt like winter had come back and swallowed the spring she'd looked forward to. And that was a new thing—looking forward. But this day, this storm, kept her safely tucked into the present and she was glad for it as her mind tempted her to drift into the territory of worry over the news she waited on.

But she refused to let concern fill her, at least not until the sun lifted above the treetops.

Her tomato plantings that she completed the day prior were, so far, doing okay. Not that she would have known any different, as she was really just looking at an array of lopsided plants. But the woman at the nursery had told her they'd straighten up in a few days. And the marigolds she'd planted alongside the tomato plants looked bright and chipper despite the fury that thrashed around the greenhouse.

She felt a few of the tomato plant leaves, her fingers playing with the delicate life. Was it okay to touch the leaves? she wondered. The world of gardening was new for her, but she was learning.

And each new thing she learned, she realized how far out of her element she was.

While she didn't mind being out of her element—whatever that meant—it had, admittedly, been a crazy idea to transplant the raised beds from Boston. She was well aware of her black thumb tendencies. But, because she'd brought so little with her when she moved to Stonebridge, what she did bring meant something to her. In her defense, the raised beds, the idea of gardening, had been her husband's love. He grew vegetables and herbs and cooked them up for loud dinner parties and quiet evenings spent at home. He'd loved the garden, so she carried it on for him.

Or at least she tried to.

She filled her tin watering can from the spigot, then frowned in concentration as she gave doses of adoration and water to each plant. Unable to help but feel like she was on the verge of over or under watering, she cringed, said a little prayer, and continued watering away.

After finishing her morning garden chores, she set the watering can back in its place—she liked a tidy greenhouse—and gave a little air kiss to the Dalmatian figurine that sat like a good boy near the door, guarding the place.

She trekked back to the French doors of her house, kicked off her muddy boots, and brewed a cup of victory coffee to drink while she got ready for the day.

According to her writing schedule, which she outlined for each corresponding book deadline, she had a solid chunk of her latest book to get through. The basic story had been set, the stakes laid, and today it would be time to raise those stakes, to stir something up. It was possible that one of her characters would be ushered out of the picture. Or framed for another, similar crime, she thought, getting into the groove.

She carted the coffee cup back up the creaky stairs toward her en suite master bathroom as her mind reeled with the new direction her imagination presented.

Grabbing her phone along the way, she checked for any missed calls or texts.

Nothing.

The night was still stretching into morning so there was no logical reason her brother, William, would be reaching out this soon. Today was his doctor's appointment to check his progress, and her stomach clenched while her mind derailed as it considered the many courses the appointment could take.

Gulping coffee to swallow back fear that collected like tar in her throat, she set the empty cup aside and climbed into the steaming shower. It would be awhile, hours, before he called with the update. So she would work to distraction until then. Productivity trumped worry, she reminded herself.

Or, it did on most days. But she was getting better at that.

She dressed in slim jeans and an ashy-violet colored cashmere sweater, thick socks, and her favorite tiny diamond solitaire earrings, then logged into her computer.

Then stared, her mind alarmingly void, at the blank screen that taunted her.

So much for productivity.

You can always edit a bad page, she reminded herself. But you can't edit a blank one.

After squeezing out an hour of treacherously terse words that lacked any real meaning or spark, she zipped on her camel-colored riding boots, grabbed a raincoat and hat, secured her laptop, then left for a drive.

She didn't smoke, she didn't gamble, she didn't drink (too much). What she did, was drive.

It was all part of the routine. Whenever she got stuck in her writing—which she was prone to doing lately—she headed down whatever roads looked interesting. The venture would take her meandering through towns filled with new sights and sounds that would, potentially, give way to new sensations and insights she could translate into her characters' world. She would venture into a café or a bar, ask questions of the locals, hoping to spark some new character quirk or twist.

But within minutes of leaving her house, Kara knew she hadn't prepared nearly well enough for the day.

Rain hammered against her windshield, hard and without any of the sweetness of the spring that had sung through the day prior. Chipper buds that had peeked out in the early warmth now bore the brunt of the late-season storm that swept through New England. And in the town she was content to call home, the people, as with the newly planted growth, ran for cover.

Except for Kara. Then again, she wasn't known for doing what everyone else did.

The hum of the engine, the rhythm of the wind-shield wipers, the pattern of four-way intersections through the residential neighborhoods, it all distracted her mind and would allow—she hoped—for whatever would happen next in her latest book to work its way out. That's just how her creative process worked for her.

This morning, however, she got a whole two miles from her house when her car—a late model German thing she'd been given by her brother,

Liam—lost power and couldn't be bothered to budge any further. It was as if it decided the rain was too much to deal with so it simply laid a line, refusing to inch any further into the brutality.

She limped it off to the flooded shoulder of the road, clicked off the engine, then frowned at the center of the steering wheel as if it were the nerve center of the car and would broadcast, at any moment, what had gone wrong.

Her first thought was to call her late husband, which quickly sunk her mood into the deepest of the dark puddles that gathered around her.

She'd let herself grieve; she'd moved away from Boston to give herself the space to heal. And over the past year, she'd taken one step at a time, put one foot in front of the other, and had felt her way through the soul crushing grief. Even though she was no longer breaking into sob sessions while trying to work, no longer gasping for her breath through the streaming tears as she remodeled her old home, she hadn't managed to completely sidestep those reflexive moments like wanting to call him when she had car trouble.

Instead of dropping into a good wallow as she would have a year ago—bonus points for catching it early on, she was getting better there—she released the lever for the hood, then kicked open the door. And stepped out then immediately into a scraggly-edged puddle that had, to her mind, manifested in physical form simply for her to dunk her foot into.

Bad luck happened in threes, she knew. First the car, then the bastardly puddle. She wasn't sure she wanted to know what the third bout of bad luck would bring her.

Her leather boots changed colors as the rainwater soaked through—so much for weather-proofing them—and provided a nice icy jolt between her toes while she followed the line of the hood then shoved it up to take a look.

Sheets of rain blew with a surprising hardness for spring, rendering her rain jacket nearly worthless. Such irony, she thought, her imagination snatching up the experience and tucking it away for possible use in an upcoming scene in her latest book. The rain had managed to sneak beyond rain gear and move into every crevice it could, finding its way to skin—through her jeans, her sleeves, beneath the hem of her jacket. It seeped in like a silent, invisible foe, ready to retaliate for reasons unknown.

She shivered, creeping herself out, and knew she was on to something. She loved her job weaving mysteries. Writing satisfied that dramatically inclined part of her that loved to understand the dancing dark and light of peoples' lives. The highs and lows. The torment and the elation.

Though in her own life, she worked hard to maintain an even-keeled peace and steady stream of simplicity—she wasn't looking for complications or great waves of any kind. She liked her quiet routines, her life. It was manageable and didn't leave the door open to feelings she wanted no part in feeling.

But she had no difficulty throwing her characters into a world of hurt, she thought with a slight twitch of lips.

Determined to switch gears and focus on her car, she poked her head under the hood and took a scouring once-over.

While she didn't know a thing about cars, she did know her brother, Liam. And she knew that, before he'd presented her with the car, he'd "tweaked" the thing to make it faster for her. He'd explained, quite excitedly, that he'd installed some machine that cut through the turbo lag time, making it more powerful off the starting line.

And she happily took advantage of that nifty little boost whenever she departed a stoplight or stop sign. Not gregariously, of course. But she figured she made her brother proud each time she sped off that starting line with a bit of sassy kick.

Liam Wyatt was a man who'd made a fortune, literally, out of tweaking technology, and he very generously shared that wealth with his family. And while Kara was grateful for all he shared with her, she cursed him, however mildly, at the moment. Sometimes she just wanted things to be left alone, for them to be enough, just as they were, so she could rely on them. She'd worked on herself—her mind, her emotions—since her husband died, to learn to appreciate things just as they were. To be grateful for small things like a fresh, sun-soaked breeze or a bee buzzing eagerly nearby.

Most days she did a good job of it.

But Liam Wyatt took risks, always taking apart what worked, knowing he could make it even better. It was his nature and had been since they were kids. And even while stranded on the side of the road, swamped by the rain, Kara loved him for it.

Spotting the little machine that was attached via various wires and clamps, she poked at it hopelessly, not knowing in the slightest what she was actually hoping to accomplish. But having grown up with two brothers, she knew that the first questions asked about car trouble tended to be, "What is it doing?," "What does it sound like?," and "Did you check under the hood?"

Deductively, there was no reason for a relative-ly new vehicle to lose power—except for when one took the vehicle apart, only to put it back together, tweaked, as Liam had done.

Taking a deep breath that puffed out through the bulleting rain, she closed the hood, returned to the driver's seat, and called for a tow truck.

While her initial instinct had been to call her late husband, what followed was wishing she could call Liam and ask him to coach her through fixing whatever he'd done to make her car "better." But he was currently in Elkhart, In-diana at the Hall of Heroes Superhero Museum with his wife and her son—now Liam's adopted son—Archer, and she didn't want to bother them.

Who she didn't think of calling was her brother William who was dealing with enough as it was. He just needed to get better, to get through the cycle of daily visits to the hospital. Then Kara would be more than happy to call him while in car-peril.

So she settled in to work while she waited for the tow truck. No reason not to get a few more pages docked.

By the time the tow truck arrived to take her cute white car away, she'd gotten in a solid hour of writing on her laptop while sitting behind the steering wheel. Then, deciding she was on a roll and didn't want to return to her quiet home just yet, she double bagged her laptop in the usual two layers of padded waterproof sleeves, bundled back into her wet jacket and hat, and caught a ride with the driver for Tommy's Trucks into town.

Refusing to let the hiccup and detour thwart reaching her writing goals for the day, Kara schlepped from the mechanic's shop to the Rolling Pin Bakery, ordered a raspberry scone along with the largest coffee possible, then nabbed a corner table and booted up her computer, attempting to keep the momentum going.

She was a handful of extremely short weeks out from her deadline and would hate herself just as much as, if not more than, her agent and editor would if she didn't get the manuscript in on time.

Kara prided herself on being pulled together and on top of things in her professional life. And when things piled up, and deadlines loomed, she became like a ferocious saber-toothed cat whose teeth were bared to anyone who dared approach as her fingers typed furiously. But even then, she preferred to hear the hum of life scurry around her, like it did in the bakery, creating a cocoon for her to burrow into.

"You're creating a puddle."

Though she shouldn't have been startled by the man's voice—it was one she frequently dreamed about in both wake and sleep—it slipped through her focus without warning and cracked her concentration.

"Ben, hi."

He set down her coffee and plated scone in front of her. "Nasty out there today," he announced, just as almost every patron in the delightfully compact bakery did.

"It is, yeah," she agreed, baffled by his arrival with her order. "Why are you delivering my food and coffee?"

"They called your name a few times but you didn't answer. Figured I'd bring it over. It was either that or take it for myself, which was a pretty strong possibility. Scone looks good today."

Her pulse pounded in thick, vibrant beats. The highlight—always—of her late afternoon was to sit in the Plumber's Pub and finish out her writing day from the worn wooden table beside the window, watching Ben tend bar in his casual, friendly way as her fingers raced over the keys of her laptop. Seeing him out of the context of her daily ritual caused a spike of panicky thrill to shimmy up her spine. "I didn't hear them call my name out. This is nice of you, thank you."

"My pleasure. And you're still creating a puddle. Here, stand," he instructed, which she did, not realizing she was still wearing her jacket and hat until he peeled both off of her.

She quickly smoothed out her hair with her fingertips as she watched him hang her dripping jacket and sopping wet hat on the bursting coa-track along the sidewall.

On his way back to her table, he stopped to grab his coffee, then greeted Burt, the real es-tate agent whose picture was plastered on signs around town, then exchanged a quick pleasantry about the weather with the local librarian. Then he returned to Kara's table, sliding onto the seat across from her.

The man should be the mayor of Stonebridge, she thought, studying him. He filled a room with his strength and presence, and lit that room with his generous smile and intense golden eyes that featured shadowed flecks, hints of dark brown lines that dove beyond that initial glow of friendly affection.

If he were a character in her book, he'd be a mayor, she decided. One who fought for the people, maybe juxtaposed against tight strings of corruption that webbed around him.

"Thank you, again," she told him, realizing she should say something aloud rather than play qui-etly in her thoughts. She'd gotten so out of practice with men, and had largely become uncomfortable around them when they appeared out of their usual context.

So much for being a ferocious tiger, she thought dully.

Well, to be fair, not all men made her uncomfortable. Just the man now seated on the other side of her table, the man disturbing her work—which, admittedly, she'd momentarily forgotten about.

"Welcome. Didn't know you came here in the morning."

"I don't usually. But my car stalled and...now I'm here."

"Well you look just as cute and pint-sized as you do in the pub, huddled over your computer in the corner."

Her spine straightened and her eyes narrowed in defiance. "You know, even though pint-sized means very small, there are some instances where it would mean the opposite."

"Yeah?"

"Yeah. Like, for example, if I walked into your bar and ordered a pint-sized martini, that would be a very big martini."

His lips tugged into a grin, making her heart stammer. The man was too handsome, she thought, as she'd thought on several occasions. Too handsome to be a single man, tucked into a small town pub day in, day out.

She'd gone there, to Stonebridge, to block out the overwhelming abundance of feelings that bombarded her in Boston. She'd escaped to clear her head, to start over after her husband's death, to live simply. But being near Ben—his smile, his usual dashes of attention—bordered between inspiring just enough emotion to keep her blood flowing, and stirring way, way too much.

"True enough. But I still stand by the cute comment," he told her. "Need help with your car? I can get a few guys and we'll tow it in, take a look."

She reached for her coffee, remembering, finally, that it was there. "I had it towed already, but thank you for the offer. I guess he needs—Tommy, at Tommy's Trucks, that is—to order some special diagnostic reader to determine what the problem is. Won't be here for a couple days."

Rain splattered in a burst against the windows, causing a quick hush in the bakery, which was then followed by the building of increasingly loud, overly excited chatter.

"Need a lift home?" he asked once everyone dove back into conversation.

She shook her head of long hair that was so dark it reflected the cool glare through the windows, making it look like shiny, delicately spun black silk. "It's less than a mile from town. I'm good."

"A mile in this weather is like ten on a good day."

She glanced outside to the square patch of green grass in the town's center. It was covered by a thick wet sheen, while the white gazebo that announced the town's quaintness hunkered down for the thrashing. The businesses that surrounded—some made of old brick, some more newly painted wood—snuggled close to the green,

seeming to nuzzle a bit closer together, as if ral-
lying in solidarity.

Solidarity, she thought. She missed the idea
of a comrade, the idea of not having to face a
storm—or life—alone. But with a comrade, one
ran the risk of losing that comrade, which cut
deeper, hurt greater than never having known
one in the first place. A storm she could handle
just fine on her own. She'd weathered many and
wasn't likely to wash away anytime soon.

"It's just rain, right?" she said softly then angled
to face Ben.

The look in his eyes shifted, almost impercep-
tibly cooling over. While she was sorry to see
it, she also wondered, briefly, what had caused
them to darken in their slight hardening.

"True enough." Ben rose to standing, taking his
cup into his strong, long-fingered hold. "See you
at the pub later?"

She nodded, torn between a simple sadness at
seeing him go, and feeling impending relief that
she would get in a full breath and a good amount
of work after he left. "Depends on how long the

wrath of the storm lasts," she told him. "But I think I'll be there."

He stepped closer to her, his hand resting on the back of her chair. The heat from it—which was, perhaps, only in her imagination—radiated through her.

"It's just rain, right?" He casually tossed her words back at her then grinned instead of saying goodbye.

Weaving back through the crowd that had gathered in the bakery for hot coffee on the cool morning, Ben reached the door and ordered himself not to turn around.

He did wonder, though, if she watched him.

The woman was a damn enigma. And even after seeing her almost daily in the pub over the past year, he still had no idea what hummed inside of her. He'd made offers—asked if she would join him at town picnics, ice cream socials, dinner at a new restaurant in a nearby town, hell, even a ride home in a brutal storm—but she always said no. And then, the next day rolled around and he figured he'd run her off, but there she was, bright and lovely all over again.

She seemed interested at times, and like she was on the verge of fleeing at other times. He couldn't, for the life of him, figure out what made her tick.

And damn if he still, like the day he'd met her, wanted to know.

She'd been married then widowed, and that had to sting. He knew what it was to be left standing after family departed—through their own regard or through death. So he'd given her time, figured maybe she just needed it, and had stopped asking her to join him, had eased up asking too many questions. Of course that didn't stop her from asking him questions as she ate her nightly dinner at the pub.

The woman had a knack for seeing into the heart of things.

As he was soaked through when he arrived back at the pub, he raked a hand through the rain that had collected in his hair, tossed his jacket on a peg near the kitchen door, and shook off any excess water on the way to the speaker system where he cranked on the music he liked to blare while he set up for the day.

His imagination punched up a few notches, wondering what it would be like to kiss Kara in a rainstorm—wet lips, heated bodies—and it wasn't anywhere near the first time he'd thought about it.

He'd been done trying to get to know her, trying to find a way in, and had strong-armed his mind into believing she was just a friendly, regular customer. But, he thought with a glance through the window over to the bakery, there was still something there, something in the way that she looked at him, that intrigued the hell out of him.

A sensible man would've given up by now. And while he was, arguably, the most sensible of his family, he was also a steady man who didn't give up when he set his mind to something. Maybe it was time to try again, try a different approach.

Rain knocked hard against the window, the wind rattling the glass, competing with The Black Keys that blared from the speakers.

"Just rain," he repeated then began removing the chairs from the tabletops, setting them back down on the clean floors, and letting the image of devouring Kara in the rain play through his head.

Chapter 2

Momentum—along with an abundance of caffeine—carried her to complete the next two chapters of her book while being holed up at the corner table in the bakery.

Only occasionally did she glance outside the window, vaguely noting the activity in the town square, while continuing to type furiously at eighty words per minute. When she was on a roll, she got a charge looking at the life around her while the story unfolded through her imagination, through her fingers. It was like thinking without thinking.

Thinking without thinking? She caught her thought and considered it. Maybe it was time for more coffee. Her brain was beginning to glaze over.

Kara did a quick backup of her current manuscript to cloud storage—her usual routine—then gathered her belongings and escaped for a bathroom break then a coffee refill.

It was a small town, and she knew, at least peripherally, every person who was seated in the bakery. But being from Boston, leaving valuables at the table, especially ones that stored her latest work, was just asking for trouble. So she schlepped all of her belongings with her, ignoring the twinge that alerted her to fringed thoughts of loneliness.

Being alone meant there was no one at your table to watch your belongings for you while you went to the restroom.

Partnership was something she missed, something she craved without wanting to do anything about it. Letting anyone get close enough meant that it also opened her up to being hurt again.

And no one could argue that she hadn't had her fill of hurt over the past couple of years.

But she was done with that—the sympathy, the sadness—and preferred the unfussy simplicity of being alone.

With her computer bag in her clutches, she slipped through the pleasantries that greeted her along the way to the bathroom and back again. She even managed to avoid getting stuck discussing the weather at length—a feat in and of itself.

Being in the presence of other people while getting work done was a risk and she knew it. Interruptions could happen at any moment. But the mix and mingle of voices, conversations, stirred her at the edges, releasing small threads of connection to tangle with other humans, adding flavor to her writing.

"You keep drinking coffee and you're going to float away."

Kara stepped forward to the counter, realizing she'd been lost in her thoughts. "It's your fault it's so good," she told Gennie, the owner of the Rolling Pin. "One last cup."

"You missed lunch but I could still make you a sandwich if you'd like?"

She didn't think her stomach could handle food at the moment. "Just the coffee."

"Coming up. You writing your next bestseller?"

"Fingers crossed," Kara said as she reached for her wallet in the computer bag.

Gennie topped the coffee cup with a lid. "My cousin Patty's kid, Michael, he's traveling through Scotland this semester. Bet he's experiencing weather like this. It's coming down, isn't it?"

"It is, yeah." Thumbing through the cash she had in her wallet, Kara noticed a check that she'd forgotten to deposit. She passed over it then pulled out a few dollar bills. "Scotland sounds nice. I've never been there but I'd like to go one day."

"Michael says it's beautiful. At least that's what he says in his Facebook posts. The kid couldn't be bothered to send personal messages. Any way..." Gennie handed over the coffee. "He got really excited when I told him Kara Keaton lives in Stonebridge and comes into the Rolling Pin. He's a big fan, especially of the Dark Woods series. And he saw your latest book at a shop at the airport, in Edinburgh I think... Anyway, he took a picture next to your row of books and shared it, telling his friends that the great Kara Keaton is a family friend. Isn't that something? I read your latest book already of course, and gobbled it up. I just loved the hero in that one. So virile and commanding, isn't he?"

She never knew what to do with compliments on her writing. It always felt so weird to hear people comment on stories that had come from her imagination. And it never failed to surprise and humble her that someone read and responded to her work.

"I'm so glad you enjoyed it. I really appreciate you reading it," she told Gennie, feeling foolish at the plain politeness. Whenever the spotlight came her way, even in easy conversations, she felt naked, as if she'd unzipped herself and was accidentally baring her soul with a stream of toilet paper stuck to the bottom of her foot.

"As long as you keep writing 'em, I'll keep reading 'em." Gennie beamed as she leaned a hip against the counter, settled her arms across her chest. "You get your tomato seeds planted this year?"

"I did, yeah. Thanks again for your help last year. This year, I'll be better at... What is it called? Pinching?"

"Pinching, pruning," Gennie affirmed. "And make sure to give extra attention to those bottom bits. If you don't prune off those branches below the first set of flowers up the vine, then you risk fungus."

"Like I experienced last year, yes, I remember. I'm really quite a terrible gardener."

"It's nice," Gennie told her, patting her hand. "It's good you keep the garden going in honor of your husband."

Kara nodded, smiled. "Well, I'm sure I'll have more questions for you. This year I remembered to plant marigolds around the tomato plants too. Too keep away the aphids, like you suggested."

"And don't water the leaves. Keep those dry. Only water the soil. That'll help too."

"Thanks, Gennie."

"Anytime, sweetie."

By the time she'd gotten a solid start on the next chapter, checked her phone for any missed messages—still none—and had consumed her coffee, she registered that the angry thrashes of rain had reduced to a finely milled mist that floated through the town. The buildings, the green, it was all coated in a soft white haze that cooled and calmed.

Kara once again backed up her manuscript to the cloud, then zipped up her belongings, retrieved her coat and hat from where Ben had hung them, and ventured over to the bank.

Her hands shook slightly, her nerves frazzled from the caffeine, as she entered the bank and pulled the check from her wallet. She endorsed the royalty check that had been sent by her agent after selling the international rights to two of her books to a publisher in Poland, then handed it over to the teller, good ol' Mabel Farley.

Mabel, God love her, was likely close in age to the industry of banking itself. She was covered in rolls and rolls of glorious wrinkles from years of sass and smiles, Kara thought. And the thick pair of large tortoise-rimmed glasses and permanent grin on Mabel's face never failed to warm her. The woman was like a great-grandmother to the town, watching over everyone's money.

The idea amused Kara as she completed the transaction, watching the woman's surprisingly efficient movements.

"You should invest this money, hun. You should invest it in some wild, high risk stock and see how you do."

Watching a woman who looked well past the hundred-year mark, Kara couldn't help but chuckle at the bit of frivolous advice. "I'm not really a 'high risk' kind of person."

Mabel offered a face of boredom as if her play-mate hadn't wanted to play. "You already forgot about the money once. Invest it, have fun with it, then forget about it again."

"Excuse me?" Kara asked. "How do you know that I forgot about it?"

"The date on the check," Mabel explained. "You sat on the check for awhile so it means it's extra. Plus I can see right here how much you've got in the bank. Invest the mad money. What do you think dear?"

"I think you're more of a risk taker than I am," Kara told Mabel, feeling amusingly dull in comparison.

"Take some risks. It's good for the soul. Next!"

At the brisk dismissal, Kara swiveled around and saw that Ben was standing in line behind her.

Her heart stammered, even as her fingers still quivered from too much coffee.

Maybe she should've eaten lunch.

Ben approached as Kara fastened her wallet and tucked it away.

"Mabel, here, is right," he announced. "Then again, she usually is." He grinned at Mabel and handed over the Pub's deposit from the prior day.

"I've always been right," Mabel declared as she busied herself, working through the transaction. "Except for those Rum Punches on Barbados. Those were probably a mistake. But I had fun spring diving into the pool in my underwear so I suppose it worked out."

A laugh rolled out of Kara's mouth and she met Ben's smiling eyes.

Before either could say anything, Kara's phone buzzed to life and her laughter quieted when she saw who was calling.

Moving quickly toward the bank's glass door, she reached the chilled, misty air as she answered the call.

"How'd it go with the doctor? What'd she say?" Her stomach clenched, bracing itself as she waited for her brother to deliver the news.

"Are you sitting down?" William asked.

A lump clogged her throat and blocked what little breath she had in her lungs, so when she spoke, it was a whisper. "Just tell me."

The silence may have lasted a second, but it felt like a lifetime.

"I'm clear. The cancer's gone."

Tears she hadn't known she'd been holding in, released down her face, the warmth streaming over cool cheeks then dropping off into the day's puddles that collected on the sidewalk.

"I wanted to tell you first. It worked. It damn well worked."

Hearing her brother's voice break ripped her heart to happy shreds. He was okay. He would live. He would be all right.

"It damn well worked." She repeated his words, letting the glow of them enter into the dark crevices of fear and worry.

"Liam's calling me on the other line and I need to tell him too."

She nodded, unable to speak.

"Thank you, Kara. For everything you do. Your love, Liam's love, you guys made all the difference. You loved my family on days I was too exhausted to be there for them. I'll never be able to repay you, or express how much that meant to me."

"Just live a long and happy life," she told him, her voice hushed. "That's all I want for you."

"I will if you will. Gotta go. Love you."

"Love you," she mouthed the words, still barely able to speak.

The call ended, but she continued holding tight to the phone.

Her brother was okay. He was okay, she echoed as she took in a breath. He'd gotten sick before her husband had died, and the thought of losing him too had loomed over her for the past couple of years.

Their brother Liam, in his usual fashion, had turned the idea of medical care upside down. He'd brought together top doctors, award-winning scientists, esteemed professors from Ivy League medical schools, a collection of recent graduates who devoted their fifth year studies to specialized research, and a whole slew of healers from every corner of the world. He'd put together a think tank to come up with a plan for William, had paid millions of dollars doing it, and it had worked.

It had worked, she repeated to herself, letting the news sink in. And hopefully it would work for all the other people in the world who needed healing, just as William had.

She shivered through another round of tears that poured from her eyes.

"Kara?"

Ben approached from behind, so she whipped around, startled.

"What happened? What's wrong?"

Without waiting for her to respond, he wrapped his arms around her and pulled her in close.

The warmth, the clean, masculine scent, the heartiness of man, melted what had been left of her resolve and she curled into him. She sobbed without being able to stop herself, letting out what she'd held in until now.

His hands soothed, his hold of her comforted. And his kindness sheltered her, allowing her the private moment of vulnerability.

"You're making me worry," he said, his voice calm by comparison to what she felt inside.

She swallowed and cleared her throat, trying her voice to make sure she had one.

"These are happy tears," she told him, leaning back and wiping at her wet cheeks with the back of her hand. "Sorry. Don't mean to make you worry."

He didn't let go, she noted. And his eyes never wavered from hers, as they searched for more.

"My brother," she began, slipping her phone into her jacket pocket, using both hands to scrub her face. "He's clear of cancer. It was some rare form that... Anyway, he's free of it. That was him on the phone. He just called me."

Ben used his thumb to swipe at the remaining collection of tears beneath her eyes. "That's wonderful."

She nodded, feeling the explosion of nerves and excitement tug tight in her entire body.

"You're shaking," Ben told her.

Chuckling nervously, she took a step back. "I've had too much coffee. And I'm just...grateful. I'm so grateful he's going to be okay."

Ben took her computer bag from her shoulder and hooked it over his, then took her hand, clasping their fingers together. "Then you should eat something. Come have lunch with me at the pub. I haven't eaten yet, and it's quiet today. Come keep me company and we'll celebrate your brother. What's his name?"

"William." She sniffed in the quiet spray of rain that had started again. "William Wyatt."

"Then we'll celebrate William Wyatt."

Halfway down the block, Kara stopped, lifted her gaze as the moment, the reality, began to sink in beyond the surface. "Hey, Ben?"

"Yeah?"

"I wouldn't have wanted to share this news with anyone else. I've been wishing for it, this news, for years. Thanks for being there today. Thanks for being there with me."

He laid a gentle kiss on her cheek, his lips soft against her skin that was moist from the mist in the air. "Anytime."

Chapter 3

One spring, a year before Ben's mom had taken off, he'd finished baseball practice and grabbed his gear, readying for the walk home. He was used to walking to get where he needed to go. No big deal. Some day, when he was old enough, he'd have a car of his own. He didn't need a fast car or a flashy car like a lot of his buddies wanted. He just wanted one that ran.

Even at thirteen, he'd had a level head, lanky limbs, and thoughtful eyes. Several parents of other players looked at him, his deep golden eyes, and took pity. Some even offered rides. So he'd learned to avoid the parking lot after practice. Instead, he trekked across the football field then through the dense collection of trees, and came out on Blueberry Lane. He wouldn't have minded the rides, but the pity that accompanied the offers made him feel worse than walking alone.

On that particular day, he decided to hang a left at the Stonebridge Country Club, and wander through the neighborhood that made him walk a little taller. Though he was filthy from head to toe—he'd slid into both second and home base—he still liked the feel of the clean rows of homes that had lots of gleaming windows, tended gardens, and trimmed green lawns.

Ben always wondered what the dads in those homes did. They probably owned businesses, were in charge of things, he decided.

When he passed by the white colonial home on the corner, he heard a voice and glanced across the street. A man with blond hair stood in front of the navy blue door and was calling out in greeting to a woman. The woman approached, and when she was close enough, the man picked her up off the ground, holding her.

Ben slowed, watching the interaction, unable to look away.

The man smiled wide and the woman laughed, the sight and sound seeping into Ben. And when the couple kissed, Ben knew he should give them privacy, but he couldn't. He'd never seen anything like it in real life.

He kept watch as the man set the woman down, opened the door to the home, and led her inside.

When the door shut, Ben continued on, carrying the elation of the moment with him. Would he ever have a woman who came to him, who looked at him like that woman had looked at the man? Would he have a place in the world that he was proud of, one where he would want other people to see the inside of? Would he ever feel that sense of warm, buoyant pride in anything?

As Ben and Kara approached the front door to the Plumber's Pub, he paused, faced her.

"Are we going in?" she asked, her fingers still intertwined with his.

"I want to do something first," he told her.

She looked up at him in question.

"I want to kiss you, Kara. I've been wanting to kiss you since the day you walked into the pub."

He watched as her luminous gray eyes let in the light of surprise, then brighten as her lips curved, almost expectantly.

Without hesitation, he wrapped his arms around her and lifted her off the ground.

She let out a laugh—a sound he could drown in, he thought.

And as their faces were a whisper away from one another, he brushed a kiss on her lips, testing. Then another, because he'd waited so long for this. And even though his brain buzzed with the desire to devour, he reminded himself to take care, to take the slow sips.

Though her mouth was no longer smiling, her eyes were, and that was all he needed to see in that moment.

He set her down, slowly, then rejoined his hand with hers. "Come into my pub, Kara Keaton."

She looked at him, a little puzzled, but she couldn't help but match the man's smile. "Don't mind if I do, Ben Roberts."

The Plumber's Pub was packed cozily with scratched wooden tables and chairs, and was lit from the new pockets of recessed lighting. Since they'd had to reconstruct the ceiling, they'd added a few modern touches while maintaining the old charm and character of the place. Its humble beginnings were still well represented—they were simply better lit now.

The original pine shiplap lined the walls, giving it that rough, comfortable look, while old mismatched brick lined the front wall of the pub. Large paned windows framed the view of the town green, the central gazebo, and the neighboring shops. And the thick plank of wood that served as the bar lined the sidewall then curved around to face the door

It had been a solid source of humble happiness for Ben when his sister started the family-run pub. He and Beckett would've done anything for her—she had, after all, given up going to college to take over as their legal guardian. But the three of them fell in step with one another and had each grown into loving the life of being a trio of pub proprietors.

Pub proprietors, he thought again. He owned something in the world—thanks to Abigail and her decision to make him and Beckett part owners. He had a place to leave his mark, and would someday pass the place on to the next generation.

He liked the responsibility, the stability. Going to the same place everyday, giving his heart and mind to the pub, to the customers, was made for him.

There'd been a time when he'd considered leaving to go to college, but leaving his family, the two rocks in his life, felt like a betrayal. Not that Abigail or Beckett would've seen it that way. But he did. He wanted family—the unit the three of them made in the wake of the disastrous childhoods they'd had—and that was what mattered most.

"A pint-sized martini since we're celebrating?" Ben asked, stepping behind the bar.

Kara chuckled then glanced around at the mostly empty pub. There was a couple—possibly in their late thirties—in the back corner, paying attention only to one another. Old Barley Bill was engrossed in a story with a man Kara hadn't seen before. And two women, both wearing sharp black suits, featuring serious faces and slick gazes, sat at Kara's favorite window table.

Danielle, who'd been loyally serving at the pub for years, swept out from the kitchen holding two plates of Shepherd's Pie, and murmured to Kara as she passed. "Shoot me after I graduate with my MBA if I'm as bitchy as those two business-women."

"Will do," Kara told her then lifted her computer bag from the barstool Ben had set it on, and settled the strap on a purse hook under the bar as she watched Ben fill a drink order.

"Guinness instead of a martini, then? It's a good afternoon for Guinness."

"A few months ago when that man who does the snowplowing in town...I can't remember his name...but he was here, and I remember you told him that every afternoon is a good afternoon for Guinness."

Ben poured coffee into two white mugs, building Irish Coffees for the couple. "Sounds like something I'd say." He finished the drinks with a swirl of cream on top. "You remember that?"

"Well I do come here every day."

"Yes," he said as he handed the drinks off to Danielle. "You do. I'm glad you do."

Suddenly conscientious for the second time that day, she realized that, not only had she been caught in a downpour, but she'd also cried uncontrollably on the sidewalk and must look as horrible as she imagined she did. And she was paid fairly well for her vivid imagination—which meant that if the outside of her matched her imagination, she was in trouble.

Plus, there was a palpable change between her and Ben, and she needed a moment to let it settle. Between the coffee, the news from William, and the kiss, her insides lashed like livewires.

She retrieved her laptop bag, clutching it for the protection it provided. Silly thought, she knew, but her work was her salvation in many ways.

"I'd love a Guinness," she told Ben. "But I think I need to freshen up a bit first."

"Shower?"

"Excuse me?"

"A hot shower. Good on a cold day, just like Guinness."

"God, do I look that bad?"

"You, Kara, could never look bad."

A heated shiver climbed up her spine. "I could debate you on that, but I won't."

"I'd win anyway. Abigail is gone with Declan on a business trip, so you could shower upstairs. You guys are about the same size so you could change into some dry clothes, get ready for the next round of storms."

Kara glanced down at her soaked boots that were definitely ruined, her damp jeans, the matted ends of her hair that had frizzed in the fine mist. "I guess it couldn't hurt."

"Follow me. Danielle, be right back," he called over his shoulder as he took Kara's hand and led her through the swinging door to the kitchen.

"Kara, my heart!" Beckett called out as he plated two sausage halves onto a heap of mashed potatoes. "You've finally realized my love for you and you've come for me. Wise woman."

"Ignore him," Ben instructed.

"Suit yourself," Beckett told her, teasing as he topped the dish with a ladle of onion gravy. "But I'm the cuter brother, so think about it."

Ben rolled his eyes and continued guiding Kara beyond the bounds of his brother.

Beckett smiled generously to himself while he finished the plate of Bangers N' Mash.

As Ben and Kara exited through the back door, Danielle swung through the door between the bar and the kitchen.

"Your brother's finally making his move," she said to Beckett, dancing back and forth on her tiptoes. "It's about time. And it's so romantic."

"Finally he'll get laid. It's been long enough."

"It's romantic," Danielle repeated. "Don't be Beckett and ruin it."

"What the hell's that supposed to mean?"

Danielle gripped the plate of Bangers N' Mash. "Just because you like to hook up with random women who don't mean anything to you, doesn't mean love doesn't exist. It's good your brother's finally making his move. I've had to watch him swoon over Kara forever. Just be happy for him."

Beckett, thoroughly confused with the rare burst of temper—well, rare coming from Danielle—spread his arms wide in exasperation. "I am happy for him. Or I was until you came in here. What's your problem?"

Danielle hissed out a breath then mumbled while she walked away to deliver the food. "Nothing, nothing, never mind."

Beckett looked around the empty kitchen, shaking his head. "Women."

Chapter 4

Ben led the way to the small upstairs bathroom, pointed to the built-in cupboard. "Towels in there, wash cloths, all that. The hot water takes awhile to get up here, so..." He reached into the shower, tugged the lever and released water.

"Thank you." Kara looked around, peeked into the deep shower, investigated the crisp pattern of white subway tile. "I love that the shower is about half the size of the bathroom. Oh, and a rain shower head. I just installed one of those at my house."

"You installed it yourself?"

"It took watching some videos online, but yeah. Surprised?" She turned and realized they were standing close to one another, the steady rush of water spraying behind them.

"Nope. You seem like a woman who could figure out just about anything."

"Except my car," she said with a quick gleam of light in her gray eyes.

"You gotta leave something for us men to do to impress you."

She eyed him over—the lean lines of him, the strong arms she'd spent many hours watching, the waves of thick chestnut colored hair. He was wearing a dark blue long sleeve thermal and she let herself study the way it spread across the sloping muscles of his chest.

Then she thought of having laid her head exactly there when they'd been out on the sidewalk. She'd been full of nerves then, just as she was now. But something else was taking over. Something deeper than that primal desire for another human. Something stronger than the fear she also felt—fear of that naked vulnerability.

She craved, she realized, to feel the utter strength of him.

The relief that accompanied the news of her brother, William, had loosened something inside of her. She'd clutched fear like a lifeline for so long that now, relaxing that hold gave way to riding the waves of something she hadn't been expecting. Desire. And the swell of it swamped her.

God, it had been so long since she'd felt a man, since a man had touched her.

And Ben wasn't just any man. He was some-one who'd been a lighthouse for her, provid-ing a quiet steadiness of easy, luminous smiles and unwavering routine. Not that he was aware he'd given that to her. But while her emotions had taken stormy rides, while she'd healed, he'd been there—a friendly grin, a compassionate glance, a casual conversation every now and then that wasn't based on discussing grief or surface pleasantries, neither of which were interesting to her.

Ben, she thought again. A man who was standing in front of her with tender eyes that made her want to curl into him.

And yet there was a strength she felt, a power in knowing that the man had been a steady light in her life.

She heard Mabel's words about taking risks echo through her. If a century old bank teller was reminding her to take a risk, it was time to take one.

"Beckett was wrong," she told him, her pulse rattling as she was well aware of what she was starting.

His eyebrow raised and she swallowed back the fear that followed the sweet taste of desire. Could she do this? Could she open up and allow herself to follow through on something she so deeply wanted—but had only ever been acted on in her imagination?

"Wrong about what?"

Steam from the shower hovered around them in milky puffs of clouds.

"About being better looking. You're better looking than he is."

Potent with yearnings, she hoped to God he felt even a small amount of what was pounding through her pulse. What if she was wrong about the way he looked at her? What if he was only being kind to her because she was a customer? She was a Goddamn customer and he was a business owner. She'd heard his words, but doubt still had her wondering if maybe that kiss had merely been one of pity since she'd been sobbing.

Relief grabbed hold of a few of those lashing nerves as Ben closed the distance between them.

Her breath held as his hand lifted to move her hair away from her face. Then his thumb skimmed along her jawline to her lips where he traced, slowing feeling along her skin.

She quivered, she knew. The touch was so new, so intensely potent. And something she hadn't experienced in lifetimes.

So when his lips met hers, gently pressing, her senses overwhelmed, combusting in little sparks on her skin.

He teased open her mouth and his tongue swept along hers. What had felt so far from the realm of her life only hours ago—desire, lust—now overtook her. Their breath, the exchange of it, intertwined with the steamy heat the shower provided.

And it killed him to pull back.

He didn't want to pressure her—he knew she'd been through a lot, he knew she wasn't one to rush things. Mostly, he didn't want to push her to the point where she'd disappear forever. It was a fine line, an invisible line he innately took care not to cross.

Because he couldn't lose her.

"I should let you shower," he told her, then leaned in once more, meeting her lips. But he had to leave, mostly because he wasn't going to be able to stop himself if he kept going; he was fast approaching the blazing point of no return. Physically—sure, it would hurt like a damn beast—but since the day he'd met her, hints of her had whispered through him. And it would burn deep to hear her stop him now.

Kara's gray eyes that were surrounded by a dark spray of lashes, seared into him, imprinting the lust.

God, he wanted her.

He dragged a hand through his hair, blew out a breath, attempting to bring his brain back to working order. "I'll grab some clothes from Abigail's closet and set them outside the door."

Kara nodded then watched, he knew, as he walked away.

It was safe to say he was scorched to his core. He'd gotten used to reining in his desire around her. To let it loose now, he was afraid it would be too strong, too much.

She was the most stunning woman he'd ever met—and he desperately didn't want to hurt her.

He heard the door latch behind him and he kept on, sucking in another hearty breath.

Then he heard the door open.

"Hey Ben?"

He glanced back to where Kara stood in the doorway surrounded by silvery mists.

"Join me?"

Chapter 5

<hr>

Hot water steamed around the cool bathroom, settling into the crevices and corners.

While the rain outside had begun to pound hard on the roof in a barrage of beats like a pair of steady fists, inside the steam drifted and cushioned the space around Ben and Kara.

He drank her in, that's how she would've described it if words hadn't evaporated in the mists. And the effect was more enrapturing than she'd dreamed it would be.

She definitely had dreamed of this, of him. Of Ben.

She'd let herself dream lavishly, and in doing so, she'd been able to ease beyond that line of feeling disloyal to a man she'd loved with all her heart. And let herself feel alive again. It'd been a winding, bumpy road, getting to that place, but she'd earned the life she felt flooding through her. She'd earned those daydreams.

And now, the dream mingled with reality. Ben used his hands to cup her face as he deepened the kiss, skimming her tongue, awakening the dream.

She reached for him, and without thinking, she lifted the bottom hem of his shirt up his body, wanting the thermal, then the white under-T, tossed away. It was his bare strength that she craved. Not out of greed or demand. Not yet, anyway. What she wanted was to feel, simply feel the naked muscle and rugged potency of the man before her. To feel his heart beating as hers beat.

Her pulse tripped when he began doing the same—peeling her out of her layers of clothing, tossing them aside, revealing her to her core.

And without warning, a twinge of something crept up and scared her. She wasn't frightened to be naked; she wasn't frightened to be with Ben, she knew. She was, however, nervous in the slightest of ways—possibly more—that this was her final nudge toward letting go of the past. And was, irrevocably, a step forward into new territory.

But she was ready for it. Come hell or high water—and both seemed to be lashing outside the pub—she was ready for it, she decided.

While Ben lowered to unzip her boots, she felt along his shoulders, trailing her fingertips along the impressive array of muscle. She listened as the zipper slowly treaded downward, then held on to him as he slid off her shoe, then her sock, one foot then the other.

She watched the gentle care he took, knowing it was for her. And she adored him for it.

No, she thought. That wasn't honest. She loved him for it. Even if nothing more happened beyond that moment, she loved him for the care and understanding he showed her.

And at the same time, she fell into a honeyed puddle of lust as his mouth trailed kisses along her stomach, up the centerline to her chest, then back down again. His warm mouth gliding, his hands seeking along her skin then finding the zipper of her pants, she ached as she anticipated the feel of him inside of her.

He paused before sliding off her jeans, his golden eyes looking up to her. And a shiver shimmied through her again.

"I've been wanting you since the day I met you. But I want you to be sure," he said, his voice having dipped into rough depths, then waited.

The man wasn't nervous, she noted, he wasn't rushed. His steady, quiet confidence carried from the usually noisy bar into intimacy, and knowing that caused heat to spread through her like a glass of whiskey tossed back in two seconds time.

"I'm sure," she told him, meaning the two words from the pulsing center of her being.

He slid her jeans over the curve of her butt, then down her thighs, her calves, her ankles, then set them aside and rose.

He scanned the length of her body, starting with her toes, over the lean muscles of her legs, her trim hips, up her stomach, her breasts, her neck, then settled on her face. And when his eyes met her gaze, his lips tugged into a grin. "You're stunning, Kara Keaton. Stunning."

And the man melted her, she thought, her heart thundering.

His jeans were still on, which meant she was naked in front of him, and a craving sneaked up. She needed him naked, she needed to feel. And while she began unbuttoning his jeans, she realized she truly did need him. She needed this with him. And she was ready—God was she ready.

And when she pushed his jeans down and away, she reached for his body that was impressively hard, ready for her. "And you're a beautiful man, Ben Roberts."

He walked them back a few steps to the tall, tiled shower that sprayed warm water from the oversized silver showerhead.

Hot water—and a strong dose of need—singed, igniting as it covered her curves and trailed down the length of him.

His hand—unimaginably hotter than the streaming water—cupped her breast, holding the weight of it and playing, gliding his thumb over the hardened skin of her nipple.

Then his mouth found her other breast and he used his tongue to tease, to taste. Lowering further, his mouth found her center where he laid a kiss, then swiped his tongue, sampling the silky heat.

Her legs threatened to wobble, her limbs feeling like lava. As he stood, her hands trailed along his skin as much for balance as it was out of an urgency to feel.

She couldn't remember a wanting that penetrated this deep, this far beyond the outer lines of the life she'd rebuilt for herself. There were no boundaries now, no reservations. What drove her now was something that he'd sparked to life inside of her.

Desire. When had she desired like this?

And just as she let go of the impossible question, he dipped down then lifted again, sliding into her.

On a moan, her body awakened to life, opening for him. Feeling him slowly glide further into the heat, had her reaching for him, gripping on to him.

And as need tore into her, the rhythm shifted and he lifted her hips, staying inside of her, and her legs wrapped around him.

He held her as he moved in and out of her in varying pulses, eliciting varying sensations, each more seductive and enlivening than the next. Then his mouth met hers for more—to taste, to connect, to feel.

The rhythm changing again, he turned so that her back was against the wet tiles.

Water streamed down along the most perfect pathways, she thought. It trailed down the thick waves of his hair, down his ears, the angles of his face, over his shoulders and flexed arm muscles that gripped on to her. And warm water pooled between them, where their bodies met, then released whenever he slid out of her so that just the tip of him touched between her legs.

Her heart stammered as her body craved his, racing for more, needing him in hard gulps and soft strokes.

Shifting again, moving so that he slid deeper, held tighter to her, her breath hitched as she rode hard toward that ragged peak. Racing, gripping, needing, she held on to the man with all the strength she had in her, clenching down, then letting herself fly.

Sensations rippled through her, one glorious wave of feeling after another, and she felt him hold on, dive hard, then soar right along with her.

Breath a mere whisper, she murmured his name then watched his eyes refocus and steady on hers.

His eyelashes were wet. Dark wet around rich gold. And something about it made the man look boyishly handsome. And happy, she thought.

The man looked happy, and she loved having been part of that.

His lips came to hers, their tongues meeting and sweeping together, feeling for more.

She didn't want him to let go, didn't want the moment to end. But she must be getting heavy for him, she realized. And they'd both turn into water-wrinkled prunes soon, she thought, her mind dipping into practicality.

And his must've dipped there too because he set her down, her legs shaking slightly as they searched for their strength again.

"You feel okay?" he asked as he reached for the shower gel.

Though he busied himself with the soap, she heard the question come from a place more poignant than he let on. So she answered from a similar place. "I feel...alive," she decided. "I feel amazingly alive."

And she hadn't been wrong about that poignant place, as she was treated to a slow smile from him; one that curved somewhat cockily, then lifted into full vibrancy. "Good," he said, coating her body with soapy bubbles. "I'm glad to hear that."

"And you?" she asked, feeling gloriously cherished as the man washed every inch of her skin.

"I feel like life couldn't possibly get any better than this."

She tilted her head, peered at him. "That sounds a bit like a challenge." She grinned as she reached for the soap, deciding it was her turn to wash him.

He didn't say anything in response, which felt odd, like the conversation had dropped through some fault of hers. So instead of looking at him, she spread the soap over the muscles of the man, rounding to his backside where she appreciated the hard ridges, the slope of his fantastic butt, then circled back around to the front of him, wondering what she'd said wrong.

Stepping under the wide spray of water, she finally looked up at him. There was something simmering in his eyes, something she couldn't put words to, but it pierced her hard. She wondered if it tipped in the good or bad category.

"You can just say it," she finally told him. "Whatever it is."

"Kara, I'm not a man looking for quick shower sex, then for things to return to what they have been. Taking a woman upstairs for a round of sex while tending bar isn't my style."

"Okay," she said apprehensively when he paused.

"What I'm saying, sort of poorly here, is that I care about you. And if we're doing this—and I want to keep doing this—but if we are, I'm not doing this with anyone else."

"Oh," she told him, at a loss for words. "I see."

"And I don't share either. It goes both ways."

Fumbling over thoughts that rammed into her head, she took a moment to just breathe. She didn't want anyone but Ben, but was she ready to give what he was asking for? Could she really take on being with a man, committing to a man, when she'd just taken her first step on land after years spent on a sea of grief?

"Don't say anything now," he told her, his voice even. "Take some time and think about it."

A quick peck was pressed onto her cheek, then he stepped out of the shower, wrapped a towel around his waist, and left, closing the door behind him.

Chapter 6

Ben, who'd left Kara upstairs to finish blow-drying her hair and to do whatever else women did to get ready, strolled through the back door into the kitchen.

He glanced at Beckett, expecting some quip about his wet hair, or about having had sex upstairs while customers were downstairs. Whatever Beckett had to say, it would be crude, he knew. Something that could be counted on was Beckett's ability to be absurd, and he loved his brother for it.

Instead, Ben found his brother's face contorted and staring at the stove in a trance. "The beast giving you trouble again?"

"Women are annoying."

"What?"

"Women. They're annoying and difficult and...annoying."

"Whoa," Ben said after waiting a beat. "When did the tear in the space time continuum happen?"

"While you were having sex in the shower. Way to go, by the way," Beckett grumbled.

"Uh huh." He grabbed a carrot stick from a nearby bowl, chomped on it as his gaze narrowed. "So what'd I miss?"

Again Beckett shook his head, speechless, motioning in the direction of the bar. "She... I mean, all I meant was... And then..." He made a sound effect signifying his head exploding.

Ben swallowed the bite of carrot. "I'm going to need more than that."

"Danielle."

"Ah."

"What do you mean 'ah?' Why'd you say that?"

Ben finally chuckled. "All right, spill. What happened?"

"She...Danielle...came in here all happy for you, and I said I was happy too. Everything was fine and then she told me not to be Beckett. To not ruin the romance of you and Kara, by being Beckett."

Ben examined his brother; he'd never seen him so bent out of shape.

"So then she came back in the kitchen and I told her she was wrong about me. That I was going to take her out and show her romance."

Nodding, Ben continued listening without commenting.

"And she said no. She said no."

"No, huh?"

"She said no," Beckett repeated, still dumfounded. "What the hell?"

"I know you're not used to the word, especially coming from women, but let's break this down."

Beckett scratched at his ear and faced his brother, ready to take whatever advice was offered—a rare notion on Beckett's part.

"First, you told her you were going to show her romance? Maybe you could've asked her to go out with you, then showed her some romance."

"Oh, shit. Yeah, that's good. What else?"

"Well," Ben continued, pleased to see his brother being tortured by a woman. It was about time. "Danielle has been waiting for you to ask her out for years. She has a good heart, a sweet heart, and when you finally ask her out like you did, it's anticlimactic. It probably didn't match what she thought it would be like. So she said no. Or," he added, "maybe she just thinks you're ugly."

"Sure, kick a man while he's down." Beckett attempted a death stare but ended up looking like a helpless puppy.

"Look if you're going to ask out a smart, independently minded female like Danielle, you're going to have to try harder than you did. You didn't try at all, and you're not used to trying. But do me this favor, don't ask her out if you're just going to sleep with her then toss her away. She's the best server we've ever had. Which makes her not the greatest target for your next conquest."

"I resent the implications of that."

"No you don't."

"Yeah, okay." Beckett huffed out a breath, feeling mildly better. "So now let's talk about you having sex with Kara while I was down here floundering like an idiot."

"Let's not."

"I'm happy for you, man," Beckett told him, then thought of Danielle's words. "You in love with her?"

Silently, Ben leaned against the stainless steel workstation and crossed his legs at his ankles. "I didn't know what love was, really, until that day she stepped foot in the pub. I'd never been in love before."

"And now you are?"

Ben pushed out from his lean, paced toward the door to the pub then circled, and returned to stand beside Beckett. "We were never really shown what a relationship looks like. Not a healthy one, at least. Dad disappeared, mom was crazy, then mom disappeared. We weren't, as kids, shown an example of what love between two people really looked like.

"So I don't know what to call it, or what it means. All I know is that I'd do everything in my power to make Kara happy, to give her everything I have, to use every ounce of strength I have in me to protect her. I don't really know about the rest just yet. But I want to find out."

At a loss for more words, the two brothers stood quietly in the kitchen of the Plumber's Pub.

Finally Beckett moved, crossing to the walk-in. As he strode by Ben, he punched him in the stomach.

"What's that for?"

"You deserve it," Beckett explained as he tugged on the shiny handle to the walk-in.

"I deserve to be punched?"

Beckett shook his head. "Love. You deserve love," he told him before disappearing behind the thick door.

The corners of Ben's mouth curved as he took a deep breath then made his way back into the pub. Maybe he did. But so did his little brother.

Chapter 7

S he'd had countless conversations with Ben over the past year. Whenever he brought her food order over, he'd slid onto the seat across from her and chatted with her while she ate. Unless, of course, the pub was too busy, or she was on a role with her latest manuscript. If the latter was the case, she would explain—with little fanfare—that she would be ever so daintily shoveling food in her mouth and typing through the chews without time to talk.

Which he'd laughed at, then left her in peace.

But even on days when, for one reason or another, she didn't have dinner at the pub, she liked to order a celebratory drink once she finished her writing for the day. The unspoken routine was that Ben would deliver her drink, also bringing one for himself, and they'd chat. Like two pals, she would tell him about her latest work, and he would fill her in on town happenings.

She'd had countless conversations with the man in his pub, so why, she wondered, was she so nervous making her way back down the stairs?

Should she go through the kitchen as they had when they'd gone up? Or go around the building and in the front door?

Clad in a pair of Abigail's leggings and an over-sized charcoal gray knit sweater, she reached the bottom of the stairs and decided to go through the kitchen. If she was going to contemplate dat-ing Ben—which would mean promises, expecta-tions, and opening up to feelings she wasn't sure she was ready to feel—she may as well put her toe in the water and get comfortable being more than just a customer.

Before reaching the doorknob, a growling roar shook the ground.

Repositioning the hold of her computer bag on her shoulder, she then pulled open the door and peeked outside.

Sheets of rain streamed down into the ground, shooting from the thundering sky like bullets racing to penetrate through sodden earth.

She quickly darted out then back in the nearby kitchen door, clutching her bag. Having left her raincoat in the pub, she was damp all over again by the time she ducked inside for cover.

"It's coming down out there."

She patted off the surface wet as she glanced at Beckett. "It really is. And it's so dark, it looks like midnight. What time is it?"

"Nearly five. The dark is throwing everyone off. The pub's jammed with people apparently wanting an early dinner, then to run home before the nasty peak of the storm hits."

"This isn't the peak? That's a scary thought."

"Let's hope the roof holds and we don't all fly away."

When she looked at Beckett with wide eyes, he laughed. He was happy she'd come through the kitchen, just as he was happy Ben was tied up out front, filling drink orders and wiping up puddles from stray umbrellas.

"Just kidding," he told her. "We wouldn't fly away. New Englanders are made of stronger stuff. Hey, can you grab that bunch of flat-leaf parsley over there?" He pointed, motioning toward the bouquet of leafy green.

"Sure. Sounds busy out there." She motioned toward the door to the bar.

"Sounded like you guys got busy upstairs."

She let out a chuckle. She'd been going to the pub long enough to expect comments like that from Beckett. And rather than his words making her blush, she settled into a sense of pride, she realized. Sweet, happy pride at having had terrific sex with a man who adored her.

There, she thought. She was dipping more than just her toe into the idea of dating—relationship dating—Ben. And it felt more natural than she thought it would. Not like remembering back to when she'd learned how to ride a bike, she decided. There was nothing backwards about this.

It was more like jumping into a vast new lake, one surrounded by unfamiliar landscape. But the concept of swimming was still the same.

Maybe she could do this.

"It's good, you two," he continued. "Ben's one of the good guys."

"He is, isn't he? I thought that when I met him." She smiled to herself, breathing out a quiet sigh. "What about you?"

"What about me?"

"You one of the good guys too?"

He made a noncommittal sound then thought of Danielle and remembered that she was bound to barrel in the door at any moment in search of the two plates of mashed potatoes and gravy.

"Know how to chop parsley?"

Kara hung her bag on one of the hooks near the door then headed for the sink to wash her hands. "I suppose if I can kill it in my greenhouse, I can manage to kill it on a chopping board too. Sure. Knife?"

He pulled one from a drawer and passed it over when she returned, pointed to the bamboo cutting board. "Fine chop."

"All right."

Watching her out of the corner of his eye, he wondered if this was what it would be like to be in a relationship. To have someone lend a hand when it was needed, that they'd be around to chat with, laugh with. Ben had been right, none of them had been raised with any kind of example of what that looked like. Was it that way for Abigail too? How did she know how to be a wife?

"I'm a good guy. Mostly. But Ben's better," Beckett said to her as he piled clouds of mashed potatoes onto two oval plates. "He's always been the responsible one. Well, Abigail's probably the most responsible, but Ben...he was hit pretty hard when mom disappeared. Took on a lot of responsibility."

Kara stopped chopping for a moment, looked over at Beckett. "I know a little bit about that but not much."

"He'll tell you. He's a straight shooter when it's important."

"I'm learning that." She continued chopping the parsley, running the knife through it again, releasing the subtle scent of fresh green. "So why are you telling me this?"

"Because I want you to know that, even though he comes across as easygoing, it hasn't been easy for him. For any of us. We were abandoned by people who should've loved us. So whatever you guys are doing, that's between you two. But if you hurt him, Abigail and I will hunt you down and kill you." He grinned brightly, slipping back into his mode of charm. "Just thought you should know."

"You're a good brother." Kara gripped the edges of the cutting board and walked the newly chopped mound of parsley over to Beckett. "I have two brothers and if they were here, they would say the same to you. It's nice you watch over Ben, he's lucky to have you."

Beckett shrugged as he poured steaming gravy over the mashed potatoes. "He's only a year older than me, but he's the closest thing to a dad I've got."

"Then you're both lucky to have each other."

Pleased with her easy response to what he'd said, he dusted the potatoes and gravy with a burst of parsley, then set the plates under the warmer. "Now that we're straight on that, can I ask you something?"

"Sure."

"How the hell does a guy romance a woman?"

Chapter 8

The familiar faces grew increasingly illustrat-ed throughout the evening. The louder the thunder banged on the bar, the more the people drank and the louder the stories became. It was the way of the storms in small town, Stonebridge—to hunker down together, to ooo and ahh when the lights dimmed and threatened to flicker out.

In loud blusters, the black sky boomed and rain pelleted against the window. It was like a firm punch to the gut followed by a series of jabs, then another knockout blow. And by the time you made it back up to your feet, the next round began and the same routine happened all over again.

Even still, laughter chimed in the Plumber's Pub, the merry patrons pausing only to blithely mock the rage outside when it was so loud it interrupted a tall tale or two.

Kara sat perched at the bar, chatted with the regulars she'd seen—some daily, some more sparsely—since she'd moved from Boston. Though she, too, was a regular, her usual routine at the pub was that of the outsider—working from her favorite corner table in the window, overhearing occasional conversations when she paused in her work. Rarely participating, always observing with half an ear. But now she enjoyed listening to the ins and outs of the feud over who would run the town's trivia night, or what constituted an important enough artifact worthy of inclusion in the official Stonebridge time capsule. And she enjoyed being asked her opinion on such matters.

It meant that she was included.

And while she was relishing the colorful camaraderie, part of her mind worked to figure out how to respond to Ben in the discussion about...them. Funny, she thought, she hadn't been part of a "them" in so long, it was at once frothy in feeling, and weighted with expectations she wasn't sure she was ready to deliver on.

"And, get this," Old Barley Bill started, leaning closer to Kara, attempting to speak in a hush but missing the mark by a long shot. "They voted Hazel Farnsworth to be a timer at this year's soapbox derby." He raised his graying eyebrows in expectant pause.

"Mm hmm." Kara nodded in solidarity. "Hazel Farnsworth, huh? Interesting choice." She had no idea who Hazel Farnsworth was.

"The woman makes a damn fine strawberry rhubarb pie, don't get me wrong. And she serves a glass of chocolate milk with it. Odd choice but somehow it works. Ends up being like a chocolate dipped strawberry in your mouth. She invited me over for pie last summer," he clarified. "Nice woman, but I'm not looking to be on anyone's dance card if you get what I'm saying."

"I believe I do."

"A free piece of pie is great and all, hard to turn down, but I wasn't there for sex," he explained loudly, while Kara coughed out a laugh.

"But I'm telling you, she can't be the official soapbox derby timer."

Kara eyed Old Barley Bill as he emptied his glass of light beer. "No?"

"The woman's legally blind for Christ's sake! How's she supposed to see when the little soapbox racers leave the starting line? When they cross it? And don't get me started on seeing the times on the stopwatch! Last year we bought one with a larger screen so we all could see it, but still. Hazel Farnsworth cannot be the official timer. I'm telling you..." He let out a sound of disgust.

As Kara laughed, loving every second of the small town antics, Old Barley Bill climbed off his stool, then tilted his hat and departed for the door. His final words announced that the possibly unwise combination of bourbon and beer would keep him from feeling the wind pound fists in his face, so therefore, it had indeed been a wise choice.

"We'll see if his wife agrees," Ben said to Kara, making his way toward where she sat at the bar.

"I didn't know Old Barley Bill was married."

"Forgets himself, now and then."

Kara snorted as she shook her head. "Men."

"Some men." Ben leaned forward, his elbows resting on the bar. "You're having fun tonight."

"I am. I didn't get my work done for the evening but I'll make up for it tomorrow."

"You work seven days a week. I'd say you deserve a night off."

Without asking if she wanted it, he took her almost full pint glass of warm beer and poured a new one for her.

"Just a half, please. I feel good enough already. I don't want to get tipsy and forget this feeling."

He stopped the pour and put the beer in front of her, then poured his own. "That reminds me. We never did toast your brother. William?" He held his glass to hers, clinked.

"Yes," she said, brightening that he remembered. "To William living a long and happy life. And to Liam, my other brother, for helping to make that happen. For giving me more time with two of the men—my brothers—I love most in the world."

Her eyes misted and she was grateful for the loud wallop of wind that slammed into the pub. It distracted her from crying just long enough to allow her to let out a steadying exhale and keep it together.

Turning back to Ben, making sure she was steady, she switched topics. "It's funny that you know I work seven days a week. Funny that you know my work habits. Not funny ha-ha. Just odd, I guess."

"Because you're considering what it means now that we've showered together?"

He grinned when she glanced around to see if anyone had heard him.

"No one's listening anymore. We've reached the stage of the evening where everyone's talking at each other, each person one-upping the next. We're fine," he assured her.

"It's not that I don't want anyone to hear," she clarified, not wanting him to assume otherwise. "I'm out of practice with all of this. Intimacy. Casual discussions in public about sex. Well, not sex in general, that's plastered all over the place in the world. I mean us. Intimacy between us." She paused, studied him. "Why are you smiling at me like that?"

"I've never seen you flustered. It's new for me. And it's cute on you."

She playfully offered a display of eye rolling before spinning on her stool toward the sudden sliding of chairs across the floor. The skids and shuffles were followed by brassy bids of goodbye and slapping back pats.

A group of six men—some of the more rowdy regulars—made their exit into the claws of the beast. On the other side of the window, they tugged each other along, punching back at the storm, making a dramatic show of it to the people left in the pub.

"You've built a great place here," Kara said, laughing at the performance that played out. "The pub, that is. The town's better for it."

"Well, technically Abigail was the one who hustled and bought the building, started the place. Beckett and I were with her every step of the way, doing whatever was needed, whatever she told us to do."

"It's good you have each other like that. You and Abigail and Beckett."

Ben scanned the customers that remained, noting both drink and drunkenness levels. It was only the stragglers still tucked around the tables; all others had left in search of warm beds and roofs over their heads. "My life wouldn't be the same without them. They've been my everything for a long time."

She studied him, marveling at the way the man communicated. He was very good, she thought, at sharing from the deepest part of himself, yet still managing to speak simply. The man meant the words he spoke.

Realizing that she was staring at him in her study, she sipped her beer, gave a quick glance out the window. Not because she necessarily wanted a drink or to check on the storm, but because she didn't want him to feel like he was being scrutinized. Her writer instincts had her wanting to burrow in and ask questions to know more, but she knew that wasn't fair. While her bother, Liam, took technology apart to understand it, she liked to lift the hood on people and find out what was beneath the cover—it was the approach she relied on with the characters she created. But tonight, she wanted to hear what Ben had to say without her prompting him. So she swallowed back her questions and just let him say what he would say.

"Our childhood wasn't too great," he started.

The thrill of hearing him continue was thwarted by his words. She'd known small pieces about his childhood, but through the lens of intimacy, she sought to understand from the new angle.

"Our dad, or dads—we don't really know—weren't known to any of us. And our mom, she wasn't equipped to be a mom."

"Equipped. What do you mean?" she asked then remembered she'd decided to just let him speak.

"She didn't really know how to be a mom. I don't think the term 'provider' ever crossed her mind. She was pretty absent, pretty unreliable. We had a lot of fun together, at times. Bennett gets that streak from her. She dealt really well in the absurd. Only... I haven't really thought about it like this, but she didn't have someone in her life to balance her out. To ground her. She definitely wasn't grounded on her own accord and never had a relationship that lasted beyond a fleck. Stability, responsibly, providing, none of that, I don't think, crossed her mind. Most years we went without her once bringing home groceries."

"Years?" Kara asked, her stomach dropping at the thought. "Years without groceries?"

"We didn't have the money for groceries anyway, most of the time. Abigail used to get day-old bread and pastries from Gennie at the Rolling Pin after hours, then bring them home for me and Beckett."

"Oh my God, Ben. That's... That's a lot for three kids to figure out on their own."

He drank from his beer, draining half the glass. "It is. But it's also made me who I am today. To change it, would be to change me."

"Then your mom disappeared right? You briefly mentioned that once," she said, unable to help but ask questions. "That must've been hard on you guys."

He shrugged, thinking about it.

She watched his mind make its way through thoughts that had to hurt, she knew. Had to sting. And yet, there he was, searching for truth to share.

"Abigail dealt with it by dropping her plans for college and becoming our legal guardian. We were all teenagers, sure, but she was more of a mom for us than our own mom. So I think it was both a burden and a relief for Abigail. Finally she could just take charge and be in charge, instead of running around cleaning up someone else's mess at the same time. I think that experience gave her the confidence to start the business, the pub. I think she figured she had nothing to lose at that point. We were at rock bottom and had pretty much only ever been there.

"Beckett had it the worst, or maybe the easiest, depending on how you look at it. He relied on me and Abigail because we, I think, were like two responsible parents to him, even though he's only a year younger than me. He's good at the ridiculous, he makes things fun. So whenever things got really bad, which was often, he bright-ened everything again. He's good at that. And it was important, though it may not sound like it in retrospect."

"It does," she told him. "I can see that in him, and you're right, it is important. Levity. Other-wise you drown in the dark stuff."

Ben nodded, his mind flicking back and flash-ing forward into the present, comparing the two. "Agreed. And I think it affected him a lot when she finally disappeared. Early on, he learned to leave people and things in his wake. And I don't mean to get all psychological here, because who really knows, but I think he's good at leaving people behind so that they don't leave him first. He's had enough of that."

"That makes sense."

As Ben adjusted his lean on the bar, she reached out, laid a hand on his arm out of instinct, out of compassion. Her heart broke for him the more he shared. She'd felt abandoned when her husband had died, but there wasn't a choice to be made in the matter. How was it then, being left behind because of someone's choice to leave? Add to it that it was his own mother and father that had chosen to leave... Her heart strummed in sympathy. "And you? How did it affect you?"

"I guess I'm selective about who I get close to, who I let get close. I'm not interested in anything that's shiny, slick, and shimmering on the surface. That was my mom. And that's the opposite of what's interesting to me. I guess I search beyond what's shown to me to see. That sounds strange."

"No, it makes sense. You guard your heart because when you give it, it's worth giving, because you haven't given it away in a million tiny pieces to people who don't ultimately matter."

"Now who's the psychologist?"

"Just a curious writer who cares. I like understanding the human psyche, the human endeavor. I like knowing the strands that contribute to and create the whole of a person. And you, what you experienced is, well, heartbreaking. But you don't seem broken. You seem the opposite of broken. It's like," she tilted her head, looking at him from another angle, "because you knew such hardship in your childhood, you've made sure to build a life that means something to you."

He stared at her for a moment, neither saying anything.

"And that's one of the many reasons you're a great writer. You understand things that are sometimes hard to put words to." He glanced over and waved goodbye to another couple of departing patrons. "All right, then. Now it's your turn," he announced to Kara.

"Uh oh."

"I'll be easy on you." Ben's lips tugged into a side grin.

"No you won't."

"Do you mind if I ask?"

She frowned, drank, a bit uneasy in the spotlight that had turned her way. "Ask what?"

"I don't really know how to ask politely, so I'm just going to ask."

"Okay..."

"I guess I want to know about your husband. What was it like to be married? What was it like to lose him? And, to use your words, how do you think it affected you?"

Instead of responding, she slipped off the barstool, rounded the bar to where Ben stood, pushed him around to where she'd been sitting, then motioned for him to take a seat. Then she returned behind the bar, retrieved a lowball glass, filled it with whatever Irish whiskey was

near, and swallowed back the burn in prepara-
tion.

Chapter 9

"I don't really talk much about it. This'll help," she explained as she set the empty glass on the bar in a clank.

"My husband—Josh, that's his name—he was an amazing man. We met in high school, got married not long after graduation. He was my best friend. We did everything together, absolutely everything. Then we joined my family's business of running dry cleaning shops. We had three of them that we ran and we worked really well together. Some people say that's bad for a relationship, working together, but it was great for us. Not that we didn't argue or differ in opinions on how to run things, but working through those things made us stronger, closer."

She looked at Ben. "You sure you want to hear this?"

"Positive. Keep going."

"Okay. Well, I guess to answer your question of what it felt like to be married... It felt like I had a permanent friend. I had a built-in buddy for life, to go through life with. Someone who would always be there and always have my back." She reached for the empty glass, turned it in her hands, looking at the way the lights from above reflected in a dance of sparkling lights and fractured shadows.

"Turns out that's not how it works," she continued. "First came the news about my brother, William, and the battle he was facing. I went to the hospital to be with him and, that day, Josh stayed home to finish cleaning out the gutters. We had a crisp blue sky overhead, with warmth at the edges, but we also had five straight days of rain forecasted for Boston. That's where we lived," she told him, frowning. "Can't remember if I've told you that before."

"You have," he said calmly, listening.

"So I went to the hospital, Josh stayed home, and my mind was wandering as it does while I drive. And then all of a sudden I remember feeling like the sun was spotlighting my car, warming me through the windshield of the car as I drove. You know what I mean? That warmth through the glass that penetrates? I remember that so vividly for some reason. I remember being so warm as I drove to the hospital that day. I was scared out of my mind for William, but I just felt such a safe heat. Like a blanket. And even though I had fear running through me, I remember being overcome with this sense of happiness. Not giddy happiness, but deep, vital happiness."

The rest of her story clogged in her throat along with a well of tears. She grabbed Ben's beer and took a sip, determined to finish her story without weeping. She'd had one good weep for the day and that was enough.

He wanted to go to her, wanted to go behind the bar, grab her and hold her close. But he saw the determination on her face, so he gave her that space. That she was sharing something difficult meant more to him than his own need to hold her, protect her, and not let go.

"And I found out later that he—Josh—fell off the roof and died at about the time I was driving to the hospital. I think in some way he came to me. He loved me and wanted me to know he was with me." Her eyes filled, tears spilled over and she palmed them away. "Honestly, it's what got me through those first days, weeks, months. Knowing that he was still with me in some way. Keeping me warm. Reminding me of that happiness."

"That's beyond amazing," Ben said, reaching over the bar and intertwining his fingers with hers. "To feel that, to know that."

"He was amazing like that. I guess that's how I kept putting one foot in front of the other. I knew I had to walk through the shock, walk through the grief. And I had to do it on my own, otherwise I would've felt weak."

"And you're anything but weak."

She stared at him a moment, feeling her heart thrum. She prided herself on diving into the heart of her characters, but Ben...he was better at it in real life than she was. He knew her heart, didn't he? she realized.

"Some days I was weak, some days I was strong. To get through, I dove into writing. I sold the dry cleaning shops—with my brother, Liam's, help—and dove into creating from my imagination. I needed that outlet, I needed to disappear into my character's worlds and pour myself into writing. And because everything in Boston reminded me of Josh, every café, every corner, every sidewalk, every room in our house, I had to leave. I had to get away or I'd never, ever, feel whole again."

She pulled in a breath and when she exhaled, it stuttered out of her. "Anyway, you asked how it affected me. And I think for a while, I was deeply afraid of tragedy striking at any time. Like the unspeakable happening in the blink of an eye, changing the course of life again. I mean, it all happened without warning. Just one minute he was there, the next minute gone. Everything felt so..."

"Out of control?"

"Yes. Yes, exactly. Everything felt so finite. I became paralyzed making any decision. Turn left and I could get into a car accident and die. Turn right, and I'd be fine. It just became too much. And the only way I could really deal with that, to work through that, was to write."

"Because when you write, you're in charge of the character's lives, right? You decide who lives, who dies, who's lost, who's found, who turns right and who turns left. It's the only place in life you're really in charge of things, probably," he said, his deep voice soothing the frayed ends of sadness. "When you're creating, you're in charge."

She stared at him, stunned. "I guess you're right. Completely right."

"You're an incredible writer, Kara. You pour your heart and your fears into your books. It comes off the page pretty clearly."

She looked into that golden gleam of his eyes, her lips pressed together in a smile. "You read my books?"

"Every one. That last one threw me for a loop. I was completely convinced the murderer was that thin, creepy guy from Oregon. Had no idea it was that couple from Georgia. They were suspect, of course, but I wrote them off as just kind of crazy in a harmless way."

"You read my books," she told him, her smile widening.

"There's one under the register over there, in fact."

Playing along, she bent down to the shelves beneath the cash register and retrieved her book, Wild Sky, then held it up.

"This was the first one I wrote after Josh died. I wrote it—the first draft of it—in just under a week."

"You wrote that whole book in under a week?"

"Yeah. I've got a fast pace to begin with, but it was my sanity back then. About eighty thousand words, I think it was. It just poured out of me without thinking too much."

"That's quite a gift you have, Kara Keaton. And while it was under really hard circumstances, I'm glad you found your way to Stonebridge. How did you find your way to Stonebridge, by the way?"

She set the book back down on the shelf. "I just needed out of Boston. So one day I got in my car to drive—it's what I do when I need to not think. It distracts my mind and allows part of it to just wander, somehow. So I got in my car and ended up driving through Stonebridge. I fell in love with the town first. This great mix of old and new buildings all situated around a big square patch of bright green grass. I felt it in my bones. This was my place, what I'd been looking for.

"And then I drove through the neighborhoods and came across this incredible white house that looked like a dollhouse, with dramatic weeping willows out front. It looked so old and sad and in need of love. And that's largely how I felt, so I decided we were made for each other. I put in a cash offer with the money I'd made on the sale of our business, and I drove immediately back to Boston, packed, and moved.

"My family thought I was crazy, moving to a place without any friends or family around. But I knew I'd be making a lot of trips back to Boston to see William and his wife through his treatments. I liked that drive time, and I liked being able to be close enough to trek there, and far enough away that it was a whole new place with new people and new feelings. Plus, when I wasn't writing, I was busy watching DIY renovation videos and renovating my house. So, all of it combined, it was perfect for me, moving to Stonebridge."

"I'm glad you found Stonebridge."

"I'm glad I found Stonebridge too."

He tugged her fingers to his lips and skimmed a kiss on her knuckles. "You survived something hard, something that scares the crap out of most people. You survived and you fought back."

"So did you."

"We both did, didn't we?"

A muffled ring pushed through the thrashing call of the storm outside. The ring pulsed repeatedly, and Kara glanced behind her. "Where's that coming from?"

Ben pointed. "I think your jacket pocket."

She crossed to where her jacket hung on a peg behind the bar, fished the phone from her pocket. She missed the call but saw a dozen texts from her neighbor. "Oh my God."

"What's wrong?"

"Stacie, who lives across from me, said she heard a big crash coming from my house." She scanned the messages. "She's making sure I'm okay."

"Let's go check it out." Ben rose without hesitating, readying for action.

"But the pub. You still have people here. I can just walk," she told him.

"In the dark through a storm? Not a chance. Sounds like the start of one of your books."

"It kind of does, you're right."

"Beckett and Danielle can handle the pub. Once I pull them out of the kitchen. And if they haven't beaten each other up."

"There's something between them, isn't there?" Kara asked, searching around for her laptop bag.

"Anything's possible," he told her. "What are you looking for?"

"My computer. Oh," she said, remembering. "It's hanging near the back door in the kitchen."

"Good, we're going that way. Goodnight everyone," Ben told the stragglers. "Beckett and Danielle will take care of any more orders. Be safe out there when you head home."

"I hope I still have a home," she mumbled as they pushed through the swinging kitchen door. "I love every nook and cranny of my home."

Ben clasped his hand with hers, gave a squeeze. "Whatever it is, we'll fix it."

She put her free hand on her belly that was alive with nerves. "We'll fix it."

Chapter 10

Wild in its disregard, the storm callously scattered debris across the drenched black roads. Ben maneuvered his SUV through the mess, around broken limbs, through pools that flooded the potholed pockets of Centennial Street.

They hooked a left onto Maple Lane, the windshield wipers working overtime.

Relief came when she saw her beloved house still standing behind the swaying curtains of weeping willows.

Before the vehicle came to a full stop in her driveway, she leaped out to check her baby over.

Having just rehashed her fear of things shifting or ending without warning or preamble, she rushed around to the house, checking the perimeter, while shards of fear sliced into every vulnerable nook of her heart.

As she sped around the edge of her house to the backyard, she stopped in her tracks, sucking in a gasp. There was her greenhouse, her tidy little greenhouse, crushed by a thick limb from the ancient white oak. Most of the frame had been demolished, the greenhouse plastic torn to shreds.

Rain whipped against her face, slapping it raw, as she raced toward the shambles.

Ben followed closely behind and shouted something, maybe her name. But it didn't register in her mind that was busy swirling with sentiment.

Her husband had built the raised beds—he'd used his hands to construct the boards that were now splintered beneath the weight of the scraggly arm of the tree. He'd hammered in each of the nails, one by one. He'd been so proud that first day he'd filled them with soil. So happy, she remembered.

She stood surveying what used to be the door to the structure, wind roaring in her ears.

And here was the third piece of bad luck she'd known was on its way. Her car, then the damn puddle—both of which were ridiculously inconsequential in comparison the collapsed greenhouse—now this.

"We can rebuild it." Ben's voice rose over the beating rain. "No problem."

She was soaked through—her hair, face, clothes, all drenched. Among the ruins were the chipper marigold heads that had been severed, the vines of green she'd—until now—managed to keep growing. And when she leaned forward, her outside porch light streamed over the demolished Dalmatian figurine.

And tears streamed silently, steadily down her face.

"Hey," Ben said to her. "Hey, it's okay." He pulled her into his arms as he had outside the bank, holding her.

"It's not okay." She pushed away from his grip and roared right along with the storm. "This is all too much. It's a greenhouse, I know that, I'm not as crazy as I sound. Or maybe I am. But it's not just a stupid greenhouse to me!"

Ben squinted, staring at her, attempting to understand.

She ducked under the thickest part of the limb and retrieved black and white bits of the broken Dalmatian. It'd cracked into pieces under the pressure and so had she, she thought, tossing the remains back into the muddy mess.

"This greenhouse means a lot to you. We can fix it," he told her, realizing that the feeling of being shunned and left in the dark while around Kara was continuing, regardless of the day's progression of events. Would there be a day when that would change? he wondered. Could there ever come a time when he wouldn't worry about teetering on the edge of never seeing her again?

His voice remained calm but she heard the wariness in it. He was just as afraid as she was that she'd end things between them. End them before they began. End them before there was hurt to be had.

Drowning in rain and soggy emotions, she faced Ben. "I brought these raised beds from Boston with me because Josh built them. I kept some of his plants going, some of the herbs. It was a pain in the ass getting them here, but I did it anyway. It was the last part of him I had left. It was the last thing he gave life to. And I kept it going, the life, the best I could. I keep planting, trying to add to it each spring. I just planted some tomatoes yesterday. And those marigolds, I just put them in the soil yesterday too, and they were so pretty."

Her tears mixed with the rain, washing down her cheeks. "I don't even know a damn thing about gardening and I'm terrible at it. But I've been trying."

Ben wanted nothing more than to hug the woman. He couldn't have explained why, but there was something sweetly sincere about her. He usually saw the relatively calm and casual side of her. She was typically working, typing away at her computer. And seeing her come to life like this, seeing her heart not only on her sleeve, but reflecting vibrantly on her face, he wanted to shield her from the hurt. To wipe her tears. To love her.

And he did love her. It was a risk, he knew. Loving a woman who'd loved so deeply before, who so clearly was working through the loss of it. But he had no desire to fight her past or compete against it. Instead he would honor her heart, honor the love she had within her. And he would honor the love for a man who had come before him.

Because he loved her, he thought again, wondering if he was doing any of this right. He just couldn't stand the idea of losing her before they even really got started.

One thing he did know how to do right, however, was to fix tangible things.

He inspected the tree branch—hefty thing—and pushed through the debris of twigs, bark, two-by-fours, and a hell of a lot of mud.

A few of the flowers and more than a few of the plants were still intact. Just knocked around. "Do you have a wheelbarrow?"

"What?"

"A wheelbarrow or a container that'll fit some of these plants? They can be replanted. Not all of them are lost."

"I have a red wagon I bought to haul plants. But..." Her head shook, full of tangled thoughts and realizations. "I think maybe I just need to let it go. To let my past go. I've been holding on to things I shouldn't be holding on to any longer." She pinched her shoulders up in a helpless shrug.

"And yes, I realize it seems like just silly plants and a figurine of a dog I never even knew. It was Josh's dog growing up, the Dalmatian. But he loved that statue so I loved that statue. And now it's just a bunch of broken stuff. I think it's time to let it all go."

She sniffed at the rain, at the emotion, and, thinking of Beckett, reached for a slim line of levity. "I'm actually a really terrible gardener. I kill more plants than I help."

Her lips pressed together in a thin smile. "I should start making how not to garden videos. Maybe that's what the universe is telling me. I could teach people the dark side of gardening. The mystery writer who murders plants."

He watched in awe as she rode through her emotions, expressing the highs and lows of the ripples. And in contrast to what he'd grown up with—his mother who'd never expressed anything honestly—this woman's raw honesty was not only damn adorable, it mattered more than he ever thought it would. There was a stability that came with trusting a person's integrity. And right then, in the snarling storm, surrounded by a muddy mess, he understood that he trusted the integrity of Kara Keaton.

Moving to her, taking her hands, he looked into her watery gray eyes. "It's good you have a past that meant something to you. That means something to you," he corrected. "Maybe you don't need to totally let it go, unless that's what you want. We could rebuild something new, a new greenhouse on top of the strength and soil that has meant something to you for so long. And we'll do it together. I'll help you."

She stood still, staring at him, her face unreadable.

Figuring she was working her way through emotions, he decided to lead the charge of action since she hadn't said no. "You go get that wagon and I'll start rescuing plants."

When she didn't budge, he put his hands on her shoulders. "You don't have to let go of something, someone, that means so much to you, in order to embrace what's new," he told her, reaching for what may be humming through her.

"You'll always love Josh, and that's a good thing. It means he was a great guy, because you wouldn't have given your heart to anyone less than that. So that makes him all right in my book. But just because you love him, doesn't mean you can't have feelings for the man standing in front of you."

Choking on emotion and unsure how to respond, she breathed deep, swallowed, and again, reached for levity. "In some ways, you guys are a lot alike."

She'd said it casually, a simple thought spoken aloud. But judging by the fierce flame she saw spark in Ben's eyes, she knew she'd said the wrong thing.

"I'm not like him, Kara, and I'll never be like him, because I'm me. But I'm also just a man who wants to be with you. I want to earn your trust, earn your love. And if Josh loved you, which I'm guessing he did a great deal, he would want you to be happy. He would want you to feel that warmth through the windshield on a spring day, to feel happy. And whether that's with me or someone else, you deserve to be happy. But I deserve to be seen for who I am."

"You're right. You're absolutely right." A frown burrowed between her brows. "I'm so sorry I said that. I don't know why it came out like that, I—"

"You should get the wagon," he told her. "Otherwise there will be nothing left to save."

At the words, the thought of losing Ben, she rushed into him, wrapping her arms around him.

His heart beat hard in his chest. He hoped to hell he was saying the right things, doing the right things. He was in over his head on matters of the heart, and he relied on his straight-forward-from-the-gut approach to guide him. He didn't know a damn thing about marriage or loss of a spouse, but he did know hurt. And he also knew tenacity when he saw it—his sister had it in spades. And so did Kara.

If Abigail were around to give advice, she'd probably tell him he should follow his heart and that everything else would sort itself out. Or it wouldn't. But either way, he'd been honest, so the result would be for the best.

He adjusted his hold of her, embracing her as he closed his eyes to the rain that dripped down his face. He hoped to hell the result would be holding Kara, just like this, anytime he wanted.

He gave her one last squeeze as a gust of wind shoved past them. "Better get that wagon before we both are carried away by the storm."

"Thank you, Ben. Thank you for everything. For who you are. Your words mean more than I could ever tell you. And I'm sorry mine hurt you."

Before he could respond, she sloshed away through the mud.

This better be what love is, he thought. He was going to be in a hell of a lot of trouble if this intensity was only a fraction of what it meant to be in love.

Chapter 11

<hr style="border-style: dashed" />

She put on the kettle for hot tea, glancing out the kitchen's paned window every few minutes as she went about the task.

Ben had sent her inside with the plants while he worked outside. He'd insisted that she stay indoors while he righted some of the mess, salvaging what he could.

She'd wanted to help—after all it was her house—but she knew enough about men to know when it was advisable to let them work out their energy on their own.

So she fiddled around the kitchen, putting away clean dishes from the dishwasher, trying not to ogle as he hefted the main weight of the branch off the greenhouse structure. Rain soared from the sky, illuminated by her back porch light in gilded bronze drops, while Ben muscled through the mess.

As she felt her way through a torrid of emotions, she had to admit that watching the man deal with the demolition in her backyard, attempting to put together part of her past that meant something to her, symbolically, her heart melted as much as her body appreciated the extremely sexy view.

A man working, hoisting things, throwing things, rebuilding things, was intensely attractive. Add in that he was doing it for her, in the middle of a massive storm, after she'd had a bit of a meltdown. The man was a saint. Or half crazy, which would've made her feel less like an idiot for keeping her feelings for him at bay for as long as she had. And for saying things she shouldn't have said.

She'd needed healing. She'd needed that time by herself, just as she'd needed to hear that her brother was okay. And, she thought, she'd needed to let go of the greenhouse garden and the emotion that had been rooted right along with the plants. A new one could be built—she knew that—but those feelings had uprooted and she was sorry she'd compared the two men.

Ben listened too easily, which made her feel like she was sharing too much, sharing what may ultimately hurt him to hear.

For all of Ben's patience, the man wasn't a pushover. He cared for her, she knew, but she also couldn't overload him with burdens that had been hers. If she was going to start something new, she would have to make room for it, to make room for new thoughts, new feelings. Just like when she was writing. Sometimes she just needed a little inspiration to open up, she thought, unable to take her eyes off of him.

Ben was right though, she knew, as she folded the same dishtowel for a third time. Josh would've wanted her to be happy. And she knew that.

Why else had she gone to the same pub, day after day, holing up in the corner to work, when she had a perfectly fine desk at home? Yes, she'd felt the camaraderie around her was important for her work, but that was more of an excuse than anything. She could admit that, she decided, as she opened the cupboard, retrieved two mugs for hot tea, then glanced outside again as she closed the cupboard.

She'd gone to the Plumber's Pub every day because of Ben.

The way he paid attention when customers talked to him, the easy smile he offered, the shoulder of sympathy he provided when needed. The man was as steady and strong as they came. That his past had been so hard, it made her want to share smiles with him, to share laughs together in bed on lazy Sunday mornings, to linger too long when they kissed one another, to share silly inside jokes. She wanted to share the little things that weren't so little to her. They were what made up life, and she was ready to live it again. She was ready to live life and share what she had inside of her with the man who deserved to be cherished.

A man who strong armed planks of wood, hammered nails, and secured a wrinkled blue tarp over the top of a greenhouse in the middle of a storm because it meant something to her.

The teakettle gave a sharp, commanding whistle and she turned off the burner without any interest in making tea.

Catching a glimpse of Ben as he made his way to the porch, she scooted quickly to the door and opened it in time to greet him.

"Hey," he said evenly, with swipes of mud across his face, his chest, his jeans. "It'll hold through the night, barring another tree falling on it. But it should be okay through the night and into tomorrow. I'll be back to take a look in the daylight."

"You're leaving?"

"I'm filthy. And, honestly, I don't want you to feel pressured. I'm here, I'm around. You know how I feel and where to find me. I think it's best if you decide how you feel too. Because I want you to be sure."

He used his forearm to swipe at the rain—and maybe sweat—from his forehead. "I'm not going to crowd my way in or compete with a man from your past. You've got to work out how you feel about me, Kara. Just me."

"Sounds like you worked out some things of your own while you were out there," she said, her breath uneasy, feeling like he was slipping away. Caught in the panic of wanting to honor Josh, and wanting to respect Ben, her mind reeled fast, searching for how to share what she felt inside.

"I did."

"Good," she told him, realizing that if she didn't know how to tell him what she was feeling, she would show him. "I worked some things out too." She took his hand, feeling his fingers that were icy to the touch. "Take your boots off?"

He hesitated, searching her face.

"Please?"

He heeled them off then peeled away his swampy socks, leaving all on the porch as he stepped inside. He handed off his jacket because she'd reached for it, and watched her disappear then return while he stood in the kitchen.

"Kara, I really am filthy. I don't feel comfortable in here. It's so..."

She watched as he glanced around, wondering what his view would be, what he would think of her home. Besides her family, no one else had seen it finished.

"You've done a great job restoring this place. Beckett and I used to sneak peeks in the window, daring each other to go inside. It was an old, vacant haunted house as far as we knew."

She'd given her soul to the place—resurfacing the wood floors, wood beams, painting the walls complementary shades of gray and white. She'd refinished and painted the cabinets, had replaced the old hardware, had hung floating shelves and installed hanging chandeliers for decorative fun and function. She'd had a contractor install a deep ceramic farm sink, and a tall bronze faucet that matched the hardware. And she'd decorated with bursts of green succulent plants—the low maintenance kind that took only weekly doses of watering.

"I want to ask you about the renovations, but that'll have to be another day. I need to get home and shower, and honestly, I'm not really in the mood for chitchat."

"Good, me either." Again she took his hand, led him through the dimly lit, sprawling house.

She pulled him upstairs, and after each of them stepped on the squeaky board she'd come to favor and anticipate, she led him through her bedroom to her en suite bathroom.

She let go of his hand to swivel the knobs on the shower, releasing the spray of warmth as he'd done for her earlier that day.

"You shower. Get warmed up. I'll pull together some food if you're hungry."

He scanned her face—his golden eyes looking like they'd had a hard, gritty day. He was a man on the verge of something.

And without warning, he pulled her closer, tugged off her sweater and tossed it away.

Kissing her with a hard rawness, her heart began pounding in deep beats that reverberated through her body. She yielded to the firmness, letting the pulse of him penetrate into her.

When he pulled back, they studied each other for one more of those beats, then each began tugging off clothes.

"You know what's starting to be my new favorite part of the day?" she asked, a little breathless as she stripped down with little fanfare. "Shower time."

He grinned—a sight that eased some of the knots inside of her—as he pulled her toward him, lifting her into the shower, into the heat.

Chapter 12

Wrapping the towel around his waist after Kara had left to take his clothes to the washer, he heard a faint whoosh sound come from the bathroom door. Ben bent down and retrieved the paper that had been slipped beneath the door.

Stay naked, get in bed, be hungry.

"Yes, ma'am," he said as he removed the towel, hung it on the towel bar—thanks to Abigail's training—and strolled out into the bedroom, then climbed beneath the comforter.

The twin lights on either side of the bed glowed from beneath gray lampshades, illuminating the clean lines and elegant craftsmanship of the room. Dark teal—or was that turquoise, he wondered, not knowing a bit of difference between teal, turquoise, and a whole bevy of other similar colors—accentuated the classic gray.

It was cozy, he decided. And it was very Kara. There were times he'd wondered what her bedroom would look like, and this was it. He was in her bedroom, in her bed, he thought with a hard punch of lust. And while he didn't know what kind of hunger she'd intended, he was ready for whatever came his way. And he hoped to God devouring Kara was on the menu.

He was giving her time, he reminded himself. While his brother charmed his way into the pants (and skirts) of many a woman, he didn't want to coerce or convince anyone to love him, or make love with him. It wasn't his way. He wanted more.

But when Kara appeared in the bedroom holding two plates full of food, he changed his mind and decided he would do anything in his power to make love to the woman who'd cooked for him.

"You did as you were told," she said, pleased.

"Once in a while. What's all this?"

She climbed onto the bed beside him then handed over one of the plates. "Grilled cheese with bacon, and a small cup of tomato soup as a sandwich dip."

"You cooked for me."

"Of course I did. It's a rainy night—understatement—and it's the least I can do to repay you."

He dunked a corner of the sandwich triangle into the tomato soup and tore into it.

"How is it?" she asked, swallowing a bite of her own sandwich.

"Really good. Damn good."

"Well you serve dinner for me almost every night of the week. I figured I'd make dinner for you this time."

Polishing off the first half of the grilled cheese and moving on to the second, he couldn't have described nearly how pleased he was.

"You like Banger's N' Mash best, when it's cold out," he told her. "And once in a while you order the Pub Nachos, but it's almost like you're celebrating something when you do. Like it's a treat."

"How on earth do you know that?"

"Like you said, I serve you dinner most nights, and when I hand over your nachos, you look like a kid handed a puff of cotton candy as big as their head."

She let out a laugh. "I do not."

"You do. It's adorable."

"All right, I can play this game," she began as she licked crumbs from her lips. "You have this way of calming people down when they're riled up. Like that guy from New Haven who almost started a fight? I don't remember who he was mad at. But you stepped in, and managed to simmer down his temper instead of piss him off even more. It was like magic. If I'd written the scene into a book, it would've been a superpower that you used. Like Jedi mind tricks."

He chuckled as he finished the last of his sandwich. Apparently he'd needed little instruction to be hungry. "I like it. I like that the fictional me has superpowers."

She took his plate, set it on top of hers and placed the stack on the nightstand. "Get enough to eat?"

"Not nearly," he told her as he pulled her close. "But you're clothed and I'm not."

"I think we can fix that."

Within moments she tossed away her clothes and slipped naked under the duvet.

"Cold, Cold," she said, scooting closer to him. "I always forget it's cold when you first get in. It looks so cozy, the squishy covers, the fluffy pillows, then wham! Classic bait and switch."

"Yes, beds are conniving, aren't they?"

"The connivingest. I don't know if you know this about me," she told him as his head dipped beneath the covers. "But as a writer, I feel it is my duty to invent new words. My editor hates me. She thinks I do it just to test her. Oh God." A moan slipped from between her lips.

Because she couldn't see him, she could only feel what he was doing. The sensations webbed on top of one another—small strokes, playful swipes, his tongue plunging into the heat, his lips trailing kisses. He explored her and played with her, making her skin tingle to life with fast sparks of wanting.

He used his hands, his mouth, his tongue to send her soaring beyond that realm of control, her hips pressing for more. On a gasp, she said his name, reached down and grabbed a fistful of his gloriously wavy hair. "Don't stop," she breathed out. Then, her breath catching, she exploded, her body pulsing with glorious waves of intense heat.

When he surfaced for air from beneath the thick comforter, he tossed the covers back—off and away.

And she pounced on him. "Well, that's one way to warm a woman up."

With him now lying on his back, she straddled him, craving more, and more of the heat. Wasting no time to touch, she slid, slowly closing over him, enjoying the silky, torturous glide just as much as she enjoyed watching his face fill with pleasure.

It was endless, the desire for more, she knew. Like sumptuous waves of glorious satin, she wanted to feel more, and more still.

The blend of smooth and hard, heat and tingles, had her taking her time as she dipped down then up the length of him. They were feelings she wanted to know every part of, every intimate, shuddering ripple.

Filled with him, she felt the strength of him, the utter strength of a man who'd been scarred by his past. A man who was offering his heart to her.

She'd known. Of course she'd known, that she would feel this way while sharing a bed with him. He'd given her so much already—the ups and downs of her days had never failed to steady again in his presence.

And now she knew him, beyond the casual, beyond the clothed pleasantries and chitchat.

They were naked—beyond the physical—together. Both of them raw from the past, but neither calloused over, each of them shared their world with the other.

And, dear God, the man was also physically naked, she thought in gratitude, pressing her
palms against his hardened, stable chest. His
body was beautiful beneath hers. And somehow,
without wanting to question it, their bodies just
fit together.

She rode, abandoning to that ripe power, leaving behind all that had hindered her. Fear of anything finite slipped into a sweet field of forever,
and she raced over that field, roaring, as she
revved harder, faster.

There were no wells of tenderness now, no gentle hills of exploration. His hands gripped her
hips, his eyes scanning the lean, petite body before him, and she bathed in the power that came
from the magnificent ride.

Kicking up the pace, softness on hard, slick skin
on skin, her body rode toward release.

Rampant with passion, with heat, she raced
unbridled toward that mysterious place. Her
body clenched as he gripped, racing with her.
And they both dove forward, into that glorious
abyss. Each pulsing with life, with desire, with

something grander than simple satisfaction that neither could put words to.

But even as a writer, she didn't need words. It was all feeling, and she was seeped in it.

Epilogue

The storm continued pounding against the windows, leaving trails of reflective diamonds to drip down the glass. And rather than leaving marks of hard edges, the sparkling wet created a safe haven for Ben and Kara, a barrier between them and the cold, Kara thought.

A barrier that allowed her to remember what it had been like.

She'd let herself forget what it felt like to care for a man. She'd forgotten what it felt to feel this good. And from her toes to her fingertips, life—the delicious rush of it—flooded her.

As her mind meandered, she watched the glow from her outdoor lights shimmy through the bold drops. The array of plump prisms clinging proudly to the glass, illuminating the bedroom as if it were their golden purpose to give light, she imagined.

Ben slept soundly beside her. She had too, at least for a while. Then she'd awoken in the darkest dip of night. It was her heart that had caused her to open her eyes, to notice the light, the life inside of her veins. It was her heart that beat steadily, heating her heartily.

And then she realized what she was feeling—that same warmth that had overcome her the day Josh died. That same rush of heat and happiness radiated from her core, and she knew. She knew he was giving his nod of approval.

Maybe she was making it up in her head—she was a writer, after all, and was paid to make things up. But the logic of it mattered little. What she felt flew freely outside the bounds of reason, and she let it.

He was giving his nod and saying goodbye.

Tears spilled down, dripping from her eyes, only she was smiling.

"You're crying," Ben said sleepily, rolling onto his side.

"Sorry to wake you."

He reached a hand over, gently interrupting the stream of tears.

She laughed soggily, embarrassed at the ridiculousness of crying yet again. "I promise I don't generally cry this much. I'm feeling pretty confident that tomorrow I won't cry even once."

He pulled her close so that her head rested on the pillow beside his. "What were you thinking about?"

"I was just letting my mind wander, really. But then I felt this sensation of warmth, really strong, steady warmth, and I felt happy. Inside and out, I felt happy. And it..." She sniffed, palmed away a couple more tears.

"Josh," Ben said.

"Yeah. It was that same feeling."

"Kara," he started, blowing out a breath. "I told you I didn't want to rush you and I meant it. But to be fair to myself, I think I'm going to head home, let you be."

"No, no," she laid her arm over him to keep him from sitting up. "I'm sorry. I'm a storyteller, you'd think I'd get to the point faster. Anyway, what I mean to say is that, I think Josh would've liked you. A lot. And, not that that matters, of course, but I kind of feel like he was saying goodbye. Or maybe I'm making all this up, but that really doesn't matter to me.

"You're an incredible man, Ben Roberts. You're your own man, not like anyone else. And I definitely didn't make you up. You're a better character than one I ever could have written. You're better than fiction, Ben Roberts."

He rolled back to face her, nose to nose.

"And I want to be with you," she continued. "I want to be with you, but you should know some things. I can absolutely promise you that one, I'm as good of a cook as I am a gardener, which is to say I'm terrible at both. I'm okay with things like grilled cheese and pizza, but that's pretty much the extent of my culinary skills. Two,

I truly don't cry nearly this much; today was just an exceptional day. Three, I write. A lot. And it's important to me. And I can be a little bit like a bear protecting her cub about it."

"That much I know. I've heard you growl a few times at the pub when some unsuspecting person approaches."

"It's true. And four, I love my family with my whole heart. But, when you meet them, you should be prepared to be thoroughly interrogated by my brothers."

Ben removed a stray hair from her face, skimming a hand on her cheek. "I can handle it. Anything else?"

"Well, despite all of that, I also promise you that I'm in this with you, as you asked."

She let the important words sink in and settle, then couldn't help but smile. "The way I see it, not much has changed. I mean, really, I'll still see you every day, but now I also get sex in addition to dinner at the pub. Pretty good deal," she said a little defiantly, teasing.

Laughing, he scooped her forward, rolled her to lie on top of him. She rested her chin on his chest, the smoky gray of her sparkling eyes opening wide, letting in the light that reflected.

"I'll agree with you that it's been an exceptional day," he told her. "And I don't care that you don't cook—that's what I keep Beckett around for. Plus, that grilled cheese was incredible. Regarding your work, your focus is inspiring actually. I think I might want to write my own book."

"Really?"

"Absolutely not. I'm a terrible writer. Even my text messages are generally misspelled. I'll leave the writing to you."

She studied the way his lips moved when he spoke, listening to his deep voice that was at once playful and sincere.

"And, while I know you were at least sort of kidding about getting dinner along with sex, I'd say I feel the same. Except I'd reverse the order. Sex definitely rates a higher ranking."

"You're completely right. Or, maybe we should try eating grilled cheese while having sex next time. See if they can share top billing."

"You have brilliant ideas."

After a breath, her smile faded as she looked deep into the golden brown that looked back at her. "I do want to say I'm sorry for...well, for talking so much about my life before you with another man. I know you asked about it, but the emotion of it was just under the surface today. I think everything with my brother, all those emotions, they sort of triggered everything, and it all bubbled up together. Not a lot of people would've been as understanding as you were."

"Kara, emotions aren't a bad thing when they're honest and not used as a weapon. My mom tended to use emotions as a tool to get what she wanted. But if you're feeling something, feel it and show it. I'm not scared of honesty. And I'm not going anywhere."

"You really are a superhero, Ben Roberts."

"Good thing superheroes get the girl," he said, pulling her forward, meeting her mouth with a kiss.

Pliant, their bodies melded together, moving as one. And with the storm that still plundered around them, they held tight to one another, ready to ride out whatever came their way. Together.

9 781944 260255